THE BRITANNICA GUI
THE VISUAL AND PERFORMIN

THE HISTORY OF
WESTERN
SCULPTURE

EDITED BY
PETER OSIER

Britannica®
Educational Publishing
IN ASSOCIATION WITH

ROSEN
EDUCATIONAL SERVICES

Published in 2016 by Britannica Educational Publishing (a trademark of Encyclopædia Britannica, Inc.) in association with The Rosen Publishing Group, Inc.
29 East 21st Street, New York, NY 10010

Distributed exclusively by Rosen Publishing.
To see additional Britannica Educational Publishing titles, go to rosenpublishing.com.

First Edition

Britannica Educational Publishing
J. E. Luebering: Director, Core Reference Group
Anthony L. Green: Editor, Compton's by Britannica

Rosen Publishing
Hope Lourie Killcoyne: Executive Editor
Amelie von Zumbusch: Editor
Nelson Sá: Art Director
Michael Moy: Designer
Cindy Reiman: Photography Manager

Library of Congress Cataloging-in-Publication Data

The history of Western sculpture / Edited by Peter Osier.—First Edition.
    pages cm—(The Britannica Guide to the Visual and Performing Arts)
Includes bibliographical references and index.
ISBN 978-1-68048-085-6 (library bound)
1. Sculpture—History—Juvenile literature. I. Osier, Peter, editor.
NB60.H57 2015
730.9—dc23

2014040341

Manufactured in the United States of America

Photo credits: Cover, p. i Jean-Pierre Clatot/AFP/Getty Images; p. xi Jacques DeMarthon/AFP/Getty Images; pp. xvi, 124 Danilo Ascione/Shutterstock.com; p. 4 PHAS/Universal Images Group/Getty Images; p. 7 Anastasios71/Shutterstock.com; p. 11 Holle Bildarchiv, Baden-Baden, Germany; p. 18 Scala/Art Resource, NY; pp. 23, 148–149 DEA/G. Dagli Orti/De Agostini/Getty Images; p. 27 Photo DAI Athens, Hege 684; p. 29 Vize/Shutterstock.com; p. 42 Alinari/Art Resource, NY; p. 45 futureGalore/Shutterstock.com; p. 49 Lucian Milasan/Shutterstock.com; p. 61 DEA Picture Library/Getty Images; p. 69 Himer Fotoarchiv, Munich; pp. 82–83 sokarys/iStock/Thinkstock; p. 86 An Van de Wal/Shutterstock.com; p. 89 Foto Marburg/Art Resource, NY; p. 95 wjarek/Shutterstock.com; pp. 108–109 Alexandra Lande/Shutterstock.com; p. 112 DEA/A. Dagli Orti/De Agostini/Getty Images; p. 118 DEA/G. Carfagna/De Agostini/Getty Images; p. 129 DEA/G. Nimatallah/De Agostini/Getty Images; p. 139 Bavaria-Verlag; p. 159 NeydtStock/Shutterstock.com; p. 163 Private Collection/Photo © Christie's Images/Bridgeman Images; p. 169 Oliver Morris/Hulton Archive/Getty Images; p. 175 Robin Smith Photography, New South Wales; p. 177 Mark Sexton; pp. 180–181 Don Emmert/AFP/Getty Images; cover and interior pages graphic elements David M. Schrader/Shutterstock.com, E_K/Shutterstock.com, Valentin Agapov/Shutterstock.com, argus/Shutterstock.com, Iakov Filimonov/Shutterstock.com.

CONTENTS

CHAPTER 3

SCULPTURE OF THE MIDDLE AGES 65

CHAPTER 4

RENAISSANCE AND BAROQUE SCULPTURE 104

CHAPTER 5
NEOCLASSICAL, ROMANTIC, AND MODERN SCULPTURE

Western sculpture can be defined as the three-dimensional artistic forms produced in what is now Europe and later in non-European areas dominated by European culture (such as North America) from the metal ages to the present.

"Sculpture" is not a fixed term that applies to a permanently circumscribed category of objects or sets of activities. It is, rather, the name of an art that grows and changes and is continually extending the range of its activities and evolving new kinds of objects. The scope of the term was much wider in the second half of the 20th century than it had been only two or three decades before, and in the fluid state of the visual arts at the turn of the 21st century nobody can predict what its future extensions are likely to be.

The designs may be embodied in freestanding objects, in reliefs on surfaces, or in environments ranging from tableaux to contexts that envelop the spectator. An enormous variety of media may be used, including clay, wax, stone, metal, fabric, glass, wood, plaster, rubber, and random "found" objects. Materials may be carved, modeled, molded, cast, wrought, welded, sewn, assembled, or otherwise shaped and combined.

Certain features which in previous centuries were considered essential to the art of sculpture are not present in a great deal of modern sculpture and can no longer form part of its definition. One of the most important of these is representation. Before the 20th century, sculpture was considered a representational art, one that imitated forms in life, most often human figures but also inanimate objects, such as games, utensils, and books. Since the turn of the 20th century, however, sculpture has also included nonrepresentational forms. It has long been accepted that the forms of such functional three-dimensional objects as furniture, pots, and buildings may be expressive and beautiful without being in any way representational; but it was only in the 20th century that nonfunctional, nonrepresentational, three-dimensional works of art began to be produced.

Before the 20th century, sculpture was considered primarily an art of solid form, or mass. It is true that the negative elements of sculpture—the voids and hollows within and between its solid forms—have always been to some extent an integral part of its design, but their role was a secondary one. In a great deal of modern and contemporary sculpture, however, the focus of attention has shifted, and the spatial aspects have become dominant. Spatial sculpture is now a generally accepted branch of the art of sculpture.

It was also taken for granted in the sculpture of the past that its components were of a constant shape and size and, with the exception of items such as Augustus Saint-Gaudens's *Diana* (a monumental weather vane), did not move. With the recent development of kinetic sculpture, neither the immobility nor immutability of its form can any longer be considered essential to the art of sculpture.

Finally, sculpture since the 20th century has not been confined to the two traditional forming processes of carving and modeling or to such traditional natural materials as stone, metal, wood, ivory, bone, and clay. Because present-day sculptors use any materials and methods of manufacture that will serve their purposes, the art of sculpture can no longer be identified with any special materials or techniques.

Alexander Calder's kinetic sculpture *Horizontal* dates from 1974. The standing mobile is now on permanent display outside of the Centre Pompidou, in Paris.

Through all these changes, there is probably only one thing that has remained constant in the art of sculpture, and it is this that emerges as the central and abiding concern of sculptors: The art of sculpture is the branch of the visual arts that is especially concerned with the creation of form in three dimensions.

Sculpture may be either in the round or in relief. A sculpture in the round is a separate, detached object in its own right, leading the same kind of independent existence in space as a human body or a chair. A relief does not have this kind of independence. It projects from and is attached to or is an integral part of something else that serves either as a background against which it is set or a matrix from which it emerges.

The actual three-dimensionality of sculpture in the round limits its scope in certain respects in comparison with the scope of painting. Sculpture cannot conjure the illusion of space by purely optical means or invest its forms with atmosphere and light as painting can. It does have a kind of reality, a vivid physical presence that is denied to the pictorial arts. The forms of sculpture are tangible as well as visible, and they can appeal strongly and directly to both tactile and visual sensibilities. Even the visually impaired, including those who are congenitally blind, can produce and appreciate certain kinds of sculpture. It was, in fact, argued by the

20th-century art critic Sir Herbert Read that sculpture should be regarded as primarily an art of touch and that the roots of sculptural sensibility can be traced to the pleasure one experiences in touching things.

All three-dimensional forms are perceived as having an expressive character as well as purely geometric properties. They strike the observer as delicate, aggressive, flowing, taut, relaxed, dynamic, soft, and so on. By exploiting the expressive qualities of form, a sculptor is able to create images in which subject matter and expressiveness of form are mutually reinforcing. Such images go beyond the mere presentation of fact and communicate a wide range of subtle and powerful feelings.

Broadly speaking, the stages in the production of a major work of sculpture conform to the following pattern: the commission; the preparation, submission, and acceptance of the design; the selection and preparation of materials; the forming of materials; surface finishing; installation or presentation.

The main part of the sculptor's work, the shaping of the material itself by modeling, carving, or constructional techniques, may be a long and arduous process, perhaps extending over a number of years and requiring assistants. Much of the work, especially architectural decoration, may be carried out at the site, or in situ.

The vast majority of sculptures are not entirely autonomous but are integrated or linked in some way with other works of art in other mediums. Relief, in particular, has served as a form of decoration for an immense range of domestic, personal, civic, and sacred artifacts, from the spear-throwers of Paleolithic man and the cosmetic palettes of earliest Egyptian civilization to the latest mass-produced plastic reproduction of a Jacobean linenfold panel (a carved or molded panel representing a fold, or scroll, of linen).

The main use of large-scale sculpture has been in conjunction with architecture and is typically referred to as "public art." It has either formed part of the interior or exterior fabric of the building itself or has been placed against or near the building as an adjunct to it. The role of sculpture in relation to buildings as part of a townscape is also of considerable importance. Traditionally, it has been used to provide a focal point at the meeting of streets and in marketplaces, town squares, and other open places—a tradition that many town planners today are continuing.

Sculpture has been widely used as part of the total decorative scheme for a garden or park. Garden sculpture is usually intended primarily for enjoyment, helping to create the right kind of environment for meditation, relaxation, and delight. Because the aim is to create a lighthearted arcadian or ideal paradisal atmosphere, disturbing or serious subjects are usually avoided. The sculpture may be set among trees and foliage where it can surprise and delight the viewer or sited in the open to provide a focal point for a vista.

The durability of sculpture makes it an ideal medium for commemorative purposes, and much of the world's greatest sculpture has been created to perpetuate the memory of persons and events. Commemorative sculpture includes tombs, tombstones, statues, plaques, sarcophagi, memorial columns, and triumphal arches. Portraiture, too, often serves a memorial function.

On a small scale are the sculptural products of the glyptic arts—that is, the arts of carving gems and hard stones. Superb and varied work, often done in conjunction with precious metalwork, has been produced in many countries.

Finally, sculpture has been widely used for ceremonial and ritualistic objects such as bishop's croziers, censers, reliquaries, chalices, tabernacles, sacred book covers, ancient Chinese bronzes, burial accessories, the paraphernalia of tribal rituals, the special equipment worn by participants in the sacred ball game of ancient Mexico, processional images, masks and headdresses, and modern trophies and awards.

Western sculpture in the ancient world of Greece and Rome and from the late

Michelangelo's *Moses* (1513–1515) is the centrepiece of the tomb of Pope Julius II, at the Basilica di San Pietro in Vincoli, in Rome.

Middle Ages to the end of the 19th century twice underwent a progressive development, from archaic stylization to realism; the term "progressive" here means that the stylistic sequence was determined by what was previously known about the representation of the human figure, each step depending upon a prior one, and not that there was an aesthetic progression or improvement. Modern criticism has sometimes claimed that much was lost in the change. In any event, the sculptors of the West closely observed the human body in action, at first attempting to find its ideal aspect and proportions and later aiming for dramatic effects, the heroic and the tragic; still later they favoured less significant sentiments, or at least more familiar and mundane subjects.

The pre-Hellenic, early Christian, Byzantine, and early medieval periods contradicted the humanist-naturalist bias of Greece and Rome and the Renaissance; in the 20th century that contradiction was even more emphatic. The 20th century saw the move away from humanistic naturalism to experimentation with new materials and techniques and new and complex imagery. With the advent of abstract art, the concept of the figure came to encompass a wide range of nonliteral representation; the notion of statuary has been superseded by the more inclusive category of freestanding sculpture; and, further, two new types have appeared: kinetic sculpture, in which actual movement of parts or of the whole sculpture is considered an element of design, and environmental sculpture, in which the artist either alters a given environment as if it were a kind of medium or provides in the sculpture itself an environment for the viewer to enter.

As the 21st century dawned, several of the methods and trends that had proved influential in the previous century remained significant. Among these was assemblage, the incorporation of everyday objects into the composition. Although each non-art object, such as a piece of rope or newspaper, acquires aesthetic or symbolic meanings within the context of the whole work, it may retain something of its original identity. The term "assemblage," as coined by the artist Jean Dubuffet in the 1950s, may refer to both planar and three-dimensional constructions. Although artworks composed from a variety of materials are common to many cultures, assemblage refers to a particular form that developed out of intellectual and artistic movements at the beginning of the 20th century.

CHAPTER ONE

THE BEGINNINGS OF WESTERN SCULPTURE

The history of Western sculpture begins with the cultures that developed across Europe during the Bronze and Iron Ages. While Classical Greek sculpture, which transformed the history of Western sculpture, was a break with these traditions, it also grew out of them.

AEGEAN SCULPTURE

Aegean civilization is a general term for the prehistoric Bronze Age cultures of the area around the Aegean Sea covering the period from c. 3000 BCE to c. 1100 BCE, when iron began to come into general use throughout the area. From the earliest times these cultures fall into three main groups: (1) the Minoan culture (after the legendary king Minos) of Crete, (2) the

Cycladic culture of the Cyclades islands, and (3) the Helladic culture of mainland Greece (Hellas). For convenience, the three cultures are each divided into three phases, Early, Middle, and Late, in accordance with the phases of the Bronze Age. The culture of Cyprus in the eastern Mediterranean, although it commenced somewhat later than those of the Aegean, came to parallel them by the Middle Bronze Age. The Late Bronze Age phase of the mainland is usually called Mycenaean after Mycenae, the chief Late Bronze Age site in mainland Greece.

The first centre of high civilization in the Aegean area, with great cities and palaces, a highly developed art, extended trade, writing, and use of seal stones, was Crete. Here from the end of the 3rd millennium BCE onward a distinctive civilization, owing much to the older civilizations of Egypt and the Middle East but original in its character, came into being.

The Cretan (Minoan) civilization had begun to spread by the end of the Early Bronze Age across the Aegean to the islands and to the mainland of Greece. During the Late Bronze Age, from the middle of the 16th century onward, a civilization more or less uniform superficially but showing local divergences is found throughout the Aegean area. Eventually people bearing this civilization spread colonies eastward to Cyprus and elsewhere on the southern and western coasts of Asia Minor as far as Syria, also westward to Tarentum in southern Italy and even perhaps to Sicily. In the latter part of this period, after about 1400 BCE, the centre of political and economic power, if not of artistic achievement, appears to have shifted from Knossos in Crete to Mycenae on the Greek mainland.

THE EARLY AND MIDDLE BRONZE AGES

The early Minoan period saw a thousand years of peaceful development. The Middle Minoan period differs principally from the Early Minoan in the creation of palaces and a palatial life and art. Large-scale sculpture seems not to have found much favour in Crete, although fragments of life-size figures from this period were discovered in the Cyclades in the late 20th century. Miniature sculpture of the highest quality, some of it of fired sand and clay, was produced from at least as early as 1600 BCE. Good examples are two female figures (called "Snake Goddesses") from Knossos, dated about 1700 BCE. These women stand with their arms in front of them, holding sacred snakes; they wear a flounced skirt and tight belt, and their breasts are bare.

Thanks to obsidian from Melos, marble from many islands, and local sources of gold, silver, and copper, the Cycladic islanders became prosperous. The Early Cycladic period

Minoan snake goddess statue from the ruins of the palace at Knossos, now in the collection of the Heraklion Archaeological Museum, on Crete.

65

is celebrated principally for its statuettes and vases carved from the brilliant coarse-crystalled marble of these islands. The statuettes, mostly of goddesses, are among the finest products of the Greek Bronze Age. They owe their charm to the extreme simplification of bodily forms. The typical "Cycladic idol" is a naked female, lying with her head back, her arms crossed over her breasts. These figures vary in size from a few inches to more than 6 feet (1.8 metres) in length.

During the Middle Cycladic period, the Cyclades suffered a diminution in prosperity and seem to have become politically subordinate to Crete. Two waves of Indo-European peoples seem to have descended on the Greek mainland, one about 2200 BCE and the other about 2000 BCE. They destroyed much and for long contributed little to Greece's artistic heritage.

Mainland Greece probably received its Bronze Age settlers from the Cyclades, but the two cultures soon diverged. A prosperous era arose about 2500 BCE and lasted until about 2200. Sculpture was overshadowed by pottery, metalwork, and architecture among the Early Helladic arts. In the Early Cypriot, the only surviving sculptures are a series of steatite cruciform figures of a mother goddess (3000–2500 BCE) stylized in much the same way as contemporary Cycladic idols, from which they may have been derived.

THE LATE BRONZE AGE

Prosperity and artistic achievement remained at a high level in Crete until about 1450 BCE, when all the great centres of Cretan culture were destroyed by earthquakes (probably connected with a cataclysmic eruption of the volcanic island of Thera). After these disasters, only the palace at Knossos was restored for occupation. About 1375 BCE, however, the palace at Knossos was destroyed by fire. Thereafter Crete was a second-class power and became somewhat of a cultural backwater. Miniature sculpture was still popular. No longer in faience, figures were increasingly made of bronze, ivory, and terra-cotta. Some of the bronzes, cast solid by the "lost wax" process (using a wax model), are very fine, the earliest being the best. The subjects include male worshippers wearing boots, tight belt, and kilt; women (perhaps goddesses) dressed like the faience snake goddesses of the Middle Minoan period; and animals, especially bulls.

The art of the seal engraver flourished until 1375 BCE. Religious subjects, scenes of the bullring, and depictions of animals in their natural setting were popular. Even the exaggerations of the style reflect careful observation of the movements of the animals and their idiosyncratic anatomy, but they also relate the forms depicted to the shape of the stone—the curve of a bull's back or horns to that of the edge, for instance.

Mainland Greece enjoyed renewed contacts with Crete c. 1600 BCE, and a rich culture, based on the Late Minoan, rapidly came into being. The Mycenaeans gained control of Crete c. 1450 BCE, and between 1375 and 1200 BCE they became masters of an empire that stretched from Sicily and southern Italy in the west to Asia Minor and the Levant coast in the east. About 1200 BCE, however, many of the Mycenaean strongholds were destroyed by fire. There were signs of a renaissance, but the end of Mycenaean civilization came c. 1100 BCE.

The Mycenaeans seem to have had more of a taste for monumental sculpture than had their Minoan mentors. Of the few surviving examples,

From the Lion Gate at the entrance to Mycenae's citadel, a road led up to the palace.

the best known is a relief over the Lion Gate at Mycenae (c. 1250 BCE), in which two lions confront each other across an architectural column. Probably heraldic in concept, this design is comparable with those on tiny seals and ivories of Cretan inspiration. Sculpture on a small scale, in ivory, bronze, and terra-cotta, generally Minoan in character, remained popular.

Cyprus reached its highest degree of prosperity in the Late Cypriot period, due to increased exploitation of its copper mines. There were close commercial relations not only with the Levant coast, as before, but also with Egypt, Crete, and Mycenaean Greece. About 1200 BCE Mycenaean Greeks, refugees from their homeland, settled in Cyprus. Cyprus escaped the invasions that finally destroyed Mycenaean and Minoan culture, but its own culture did not last much longer. By 1050 BCE, for reasons that are unclear, it, too, had ceased to exist.

As in Crete, large-scale sculpture was rejected in favour of small-scale work. A bronze figure of a horned god (shortly after 1200 BCE) from Enkomi shows a successful blend of Mycenaean and Cypriot elements. A good example of these characteristics is a carved ivory gaming box, also from Enkomi, whose style shows a blend of Mycenaean and Middle Eastern motifs.

EARLY SCULPTURE OF THE WESTERN MEDITERRANEAN

Though to a lesser degree than were central and northern Europe, the western Mediterranean was considerably behind the eastern Mediterranean, where civilization, the arts, and writing were born much earlier.

The Chalcolithic (Copper-Stone) era began in Spain at the end of the 3rd millennium BCE at Los Millares, near Almería, and in Italy at the beginning of the 2nd millennium with the Remedello civilization. Bronze appeared not long afterward, around 1800 BCE, in Italy and Sardinia. The Bronze Age in Italy gave way to the Iron Age at the beginning of the 1st millennium BCE, but elsewhere, as in Sardinia or Spain, it lasted longer. The Iron Age flourished on the Illyrian coasts and in Italy from 900 to 800 BCE; it also lasted varying lengths of time according to locale. After this, one may speak of the civilizations of Magna Graecia, of Rome, or of Etruria.

During the metal ages, popular migrations, commerce, and wars increased, which resulted in the rise of cities and of fortified works for their protection and defense, such as the talayots (round or quadrangular towers) of the Balearic Isles and the nuraghi (round towers) of Sardinia. With respect to the plastic arts, one particularly remarkable phenomenon was the birth and multiplication of megalithic human representations, which gained in number and importance from the 3rd to the 1st millennium BCE. The Neolithic monuments, menhirs (single, vertical megaliths) and dolmens (structures of two vertical stones capped by a horizontal one), which had arisen in the megalithic era, continued to appear in the Copper and Bronze Ages, but then—here and there in Spain, Sardinia, Corsica, Liguria, and in the south of France—stelae-menhirs (carved or inscribed stone slabs used for commemorative purposes), like the stammerings of Western figure sculpture, imitated the human form. They maintained certain stylistic relations with rock engravings of mountainous regions, such as the Val Camonica.

SARDINIA AND CORSICA

The nuraghic civilization had an original sculpture expressed in a large production of bronze statuettes, about 500 of which have been found in nuraghi, temples, houses, and tombs. These figurines represent all classes of the proto-Sardinian populations—military chiefs, soldiers, priests, and women, as well as heroes and gods—in what seems to the modern viewer to be an engagingly direct but also sophisticated geometric style.

Corsican menhir, or stela, statuary constitutes a group of special interest. The

IBERIA

Whether in the form of great statuary or small votive images, Iberian figurative art was essentially religious and intended to represent sacred animals, deities, and their worshippers. Although much influenced by Greek and other sources, these works are vigorous and original, as may be seen from *La dama de Elche* and *La dama de Cerro de los Santos* in the Museo Arqueológico Nacional at Madrid. In the latter, a hieratic visage, with a severity not unlike some of the ideal heads of classical Greece, is adorned with a superabundance of heavy Iberian jewels.

La dama de Elche was originally polychrome, or brightly painted.

stone is imbued with life by a sculptural art that involves roughing-in of the head, animation of the upper portion of the body, and placement of a few elements of ornamentation or weaponry (sculpted in relief or, more rarely, engraved) on the schematically anthropomorphic image. These primitive statues are masculine and, no doubt, represent family or tribal heads made heroic or divine. This megalithic stela statuary art appears not only on Corsica but also in various other countries and regions of the western Mediterranean, including Spain, Sardinia, Liguria, and, in southern France, Provence, Aveyron, Hérault, and Gard, though to a lesser degree. The advance of this type of megalithic sculptural art is difficult to follow, but it is clear that these different groups are related, with close affinities existing between the stelae-menhirs of Corsica and those of the Ligurian coast. Such art is everywhere the expression of a patriarchal society seeking to impose on men's vision, massively and not without grandeur, the image of the departed ancestors.

ITALY

From the Bronze Age of far northern Italy there survives an exceptional collection of rock engravings, a remarkable extension of an art that had been represented in the prehistoric era and had not yet vanished completely.

About 20,000 rock engravings have been found in the Val Camonica, north of the town of Brescia. This art is found again further west, in the Maritime Alps of France on Monte Bego. What is exceptional about the carvings of the Val Camonica is that they represent a variety of subjects—rituals, battles, hunting, and daily labour—and that these were treated as compositions.

Although engraving played a minor role in the case of the menhir statuary mentioned earlier, relations do exist between the sculpted works and the Camunian images of Monte Bego. The same representations of collar torques appear on the menhir statuary of Gard, Aveyron, and Tarn, on the one hand, and on certain monumental engravings of the Val Camonica, on the other. Some kind of relationship thus unites the arts of rock engraving and stela statuary in the Bronze Age.

The Italian peninsula, which in the Bronze Age had been only one among many centres of civilization, took on a special importance in the Iron Age. Widespread and powerful cultural and artistic centres grew up there, first in the Villanovan civilization and later in the Etruscan; their influence was disseminated into the surrounding areas.

At the beginning of the 1st millennium BCE there began to develop in the Po plain, in Tuscany, Latium, and some areas of Lucania, a new cremating civilization, which draws its name from that of the Villanova necropolis, discovered near Bologna. It is obviously related to the so-called Urnfield civilization that, at the end of the Bronze Age and beginning of the Iron Age, extended over central and eastern Europe and had developed a metal art with geometric and abstract ornamentation. The ashes of the dead were placed in urns thrust in level with the soil. From the Urnfield civilization arose two others: the Hallstatt civilization, which spread into the Balkans, northern and central Europe, and France, beyond the Pyrenees; and in Italy the Villanovan civilization and the civilizations that, to the east and west of the Po plain, were related to it, the so-called Golasecca civilization in the great lakes region and the Este civilization in the Venice area.

The cinerary urn, which was made first of terra-cotta and later of bronze, assumes, by its form, a symbolic value. Biconical in form and covered with an overturned cup, later with a helmet, it schematically represents the appearance of the human body. Sometimes, as in examples from Latium and Tuscany, the funerary vessel is in the form of a hut or cabin—the house of the dead person whose remains it holds. The ornamentation, painted or engraved on the vases and engraved or in relief on metal objects, is in a geometric, nonfigurative style. Human or animal forms appear only rarely—in the decoration of small utilitarian objects such as vase handles and horse bits. It is a severe art, therefore, which essentially limits itself to linear exercises. Even motifs such as the disk, the solar boat, and the birds that encircle them, inherited from a more distant past and possessing primitively religious value, take on a stylized air and become abstract figures.

A naturalistic note is provided by the imagery that decorates, in zones of superimposed relief, bronze vessels called situlae, a kind of pail found in Eastern countries and in the eastern Alps. These situlae were made in Venetian workshops in particular and were very popular in the neighbouring areas. They rapidly underwent an Etruscan influence, however, that tended to give prominence in the chased ornamentation to human figures at feasts, games, or funerals, as in the masterpiece known from the place of its discovery as the Certosa Situla.

Etruria, Latium, and the Faliscan districts fall into three main areas of artistic production: northern, central, and southern, each centred upon cities with a distinctive artistic style. In the southern areas the chief centres were Caere and Veii, in which the Etruscan style most closely approached the Greek. In central Etruria, Vulci was evidently the leading art centre, although Tarquinia was unsurpassed in the beauty of its wall paintings. There were several potteries in Vulci, and the greater part of the central Etruscan bronzes, artistically the best, were produced there. The north was dominated by Clusium, although Perugia seems to have been important along with lesser centres at Volterra and Fiesole.

The very earliest examples of Etruscan statuary are flat, rectilinear figurines from Vetulonia and Capodimonte di Bolsena. These figures occur in later contexts in the Regolini-Galassi and Bernardini tombs, both of which contain pieces in a more advanced style that cannot have developed much later. These are statuettes of women with pigtails and long skirts depicted in a manner that suggests a north Syria influence, although this female type, frequently copied in ivory and amber, is certainly of local origin.

The earliest evidence of Greek influence is the presence of centaurs, perhaps transmitted on Corinthian vases. Their style in Etruria is Orientalizing, with a slim body and elongated legs, perhaps reflecting Cretan influence. These and other mythical creatures found great favour with the Vulci stonemasons. To archaic works of early Etruscan sculpture certain Greek parallels can be found in the late 7th and early 6th centuries, and in general characteristics the works still followed the Greek Archaic Daedalic tradition. The next change in style took place c. 550 BCE, when art became distinctively Ionian. These new influences can be seen earliest in such pieces of bronze work as the Loeb Tripod from San Valentino near Perugia, but they soon become apparent also in the relief designs on *bucchero pesante* (heavily embossed black pottery) and in architectural reliefs like those from Tarquinia. By the end of the 6th century BCE Veii possessed an excellent school of terra-cotta sculptures in Ionian styles. The statues of Apollo and of a votaress suckling a child are elaborately stylized in features, draperies, and muscles. Clay statuary, still retaining traces of former painting, was made in many Etruscan centres. Examples in the more mature classical style that began in the last quarter of the 5th century are the satyr-and-maiden groups from Satricum (modern Conca). These pieces of statuary were designed to stand on temple roofs, and the socketed bases by which they were fixed have survived. Terra-cotta sculpture was also used for antefixes for these temples but above all for funerary sculpture. Sarcophagi with the sculptured figures of the husband and his wife reclining on the lids seem to have begun late in the 6th century, the date of the haunting sarcophagus from Caere.

Bronze sculptures were also produced, including the *Chimera* from Arezzo and or the so-called *Mars of Todi* of the early 4th century BCE. In spite of great achievements in sculpture in the round, most of what has survived is in low relief, and a series of fine 6th–5th-century relief sarcophagi from Clusium, depicting dances, funeral games and banquets, or the journey of the dead to the underworld, are a major source of information on Etruscan everyday life.

The Museo Archeologico, in Florence, is now home to the *Chimera* of Arezzo. The mythical animal it shows is part lion, part snake, and part goat.

Superbly carved gravestones of the late mid-6th century are known from Clusium and Settimello, but the disk- and horseshoe-shaped gravestones of the Bologna, Fiesole, and Populonia graves have crude reliefs.

Sculpture developed but did not seek, as in Greece, to represent the idealized body of athletes and gods, attempting instead to represent the figure and features of the deceased. There was a continuing taste for real or fantastic animals such as lions, panthers, and sphinxes, and the Etruscan imagination seems to have been haunted by these beasts and demons, the vigilant guardians of the tombs.

ANCIENT GREEK SCULPTURE

Greek art no doubt owed much indirectly to the Minoan-Mycenaean civilization, which disintegrated at the end of the 2nd millennium BCE, partly under the impact of a series of invasions from the Balkans. The period covered by this section, however, begins about 900 BCE with the kaleidoscopic rearrangement of invaders and earlier inhabitants into a new pattern, which was followed by a steady artistic development—continuing without interruption down to the conquest of Greece by Rome in 146 BCE. Even this diverted, rather than interrupted, the flow, and Greek artists continued to be predominant under the Roman Empire and beyond that into the Byzantine. But after Greece had become a Roman province, Greek art fell increasingly under the patronage of Romans and was devoted either to expressing Roman ideals or to reproducing older works of art. It is therefore reasonable to regard the later years of the

1st century BCE, when the Roman Empire was forming, as the later limit of the period.

GEOMETRIC PERIOD

In the 9th century BCE, Greece was settling down again after upheavals and migrations both into and out of the mainland. It seems that invaders from the north brought with them the germs of an artistic style that developed into the Greek Geometric tradition.

In addition to the pottery, the Geometric period produced some terra-cottas and many small bronzes. The bronzes tended to be flat at first but became more solid and less angular as casting direct from wax models superseded cutting from bronze plates. Birds and other animals, especially horses, were popular and often admirably done; men, perhaps because their form commanded less imaginative interest, were not so successfully rendered; in the later stages of geometric art, groups of some complexity were attempted—a doe with her fawn, a man fighting (or greeting) a centaur, even a lion hunt complete with dogs.

ORIENTALIZING PERIOD

Sculpture of the Orientalizing period was profoundly affected by technical and stylistic influences from the East. In about 700 BCE, the Greeks learned from their Eastern neighbours how to use molds to mass-produce clay relief plaques. Widely adopted, this technique helped to establish in Greece a stereotyped convention for figure representation, even in freestanding, unmolded sculptures, and a strong Eastern stylistic influence ensured that the convention was Oriental in flavour—in most cases a frontal pose with stiff patterned hair and drapery rendered in a strictly decorative manner. The adoption of this convention, which has come to be known as Daedalic style (after Daedalus, the legendary craftsman of Crete, where the style especially flourished), put an end to the development of naturalism and freedom in miniature sculptures that had shown promise in the Geometric period and eventually became representative of even major Greek sculpture in the mid-7th century BCE.

In about 640 BCE, however, a second Eastern influence began to be felt. As with the gigantic architecture of Egypt, the Greeks were impressed with the monumentality of Egyptian statuary, larger than life-size and executed in hard stone instead of the limestone, clay, or wood to which the Greeks had been accustomed. The Greeks learned the techniques of handling the harder stone in Egypt, and at home they turned to the fine white marble of the Cyclades islands (mainly Paros and Naxos) for their materials. It was at this time that the first truly monumental examples of Greek sculpture appeared. The idiom and proportions were at first still Daedalic.

By about 630 BCE, first in the islands and later in mainland Greece, they were carving freestanding figures of naked men that were copies of types formerly seen only in minor art and that owed something in proportion and details of pose to the common Egyptian standing figures. This new series of life-size or larger marble youths (kouroi) reveals rapid developments in technique and style, notably a transition from the Daedalic past to greater naturalism through the new monumental manner. The earliest of these figures were, as might be expected, dedications in sanctuaries, especially on the island of Delos, but some were grave markers, as on another island, Thera. At the same time, the older style was used for relief decoration of temples in Crete and Greece, particularly at Mycenae.

ARCHAIC PERIOD

The kouroi, which had become standardized as freestanding statues of naked youths with hands to sides and one leg advanced, were the most representative examples of Archaic sculpture. At first their proportions were based on theory rather than observation; much the same was true of the anatomical details, which were treated as separate

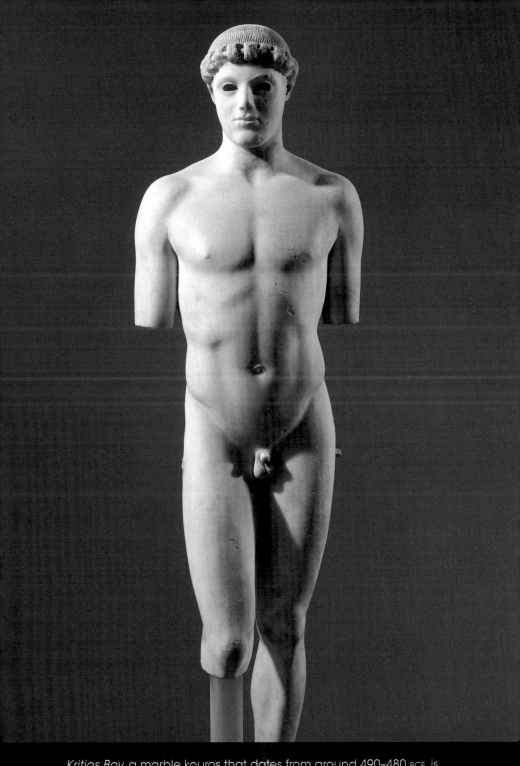

Kritios Boy, a marble kouros that dates from around 490–480 BCE, is now in the collection of the Acropolis Museum, in Athens.

patterns applied to the figure with no proper understanding of their physiological relationships. Growing awareness of natural forms, although still without systematic study of the model, together with technical mastery, led to a realism that is striking in comparison with the Daedalic pieces of the Orientalizing period.

Still, the overriding considerations of proportion and pattern were never subordinated to nature. Only in the years just before the Persian invasion of 480 BCE did some sculptors recognize the organic structure of the body and succeed in showing a truly relaxed pose, with the weight shifted onto one leg and the hips and torso consequently tilted to break the rigid symmetry of the characteristic kouros of the Archaic period

In the female counterpart of the kouros, the kore, Archaic sculptors were again preoccupied with proportion and pattern—the pattern of drapery rather than of anatomy. Ionian (Chios, Samos) and island (Naxos) sculptors took the lead in developing decorative schemes for rendering the fall and splay of the folds of the loosely draped Ionic dress (*chiton*) and overmantle (*himation*). These patterns, like the anatomy of the kouroi, suggest nature rather than copy it; the strict logic of dressmaking is never observed by the sculptor, who uses the natural gesture of pulling a long skirt up and to one side first to produce a pleasing pattern of folds and only later to reveal the contours of the legs and body beneath. Most of the korai, like the kouroi, stood as dedications in sanctuaries, the richest series being from the Acropolis at Athens (these were overthrown by the Persians and then piously buried by the returning Athenians).

In the addition of sculpture to architecture, the determining factor was usually its position on the building. On a Doric temple, for instance, the metope frieze offered a series of rectangular plaques for reliefs that could accommodate two or three figures. There was a tendency in the Archaic period to let the action run on from one metope to the next, regardless of the intervening triglyph, a practice that was later abandoned. Above the frieze, the pediments formed by the gabled roof provided an awkward field—a long, low triangle. The sculptors of early temple pediments met the problem by depicting separate groups of different sizes, as at Corcyra, or by devising monster bodies to fill the shallow corners, as in Athens. Later, the advantages of using fighting groups with falling and fallen bodies were discovered; this type is represented at Athens and Aegina. The later Archaic pedimental figures were executed virtually in the round, standing against or just free from the background of the gable. Because these figures, unlike the kouroi and korai, were often in violent action, it may have been through meeting the problems of architectural sculpture that the artist arrived at a better understanding of the dynamics of the human body.

Work in relief also was used on gravestones, chiefly in Athens, for decorative bases of columns and for the frieze decoration on Ionic buildings, of which the best examples are from the Siphnian Treasury at Delphi, constructed shortly before 525 BCE. The shallow relief on these works is little more than drawing rendered partly in the round; but the sculptor soon learned how, even in the shallowest relief, to indicate depth by overlapping figures and by bringing details up into the front plane. A dark-painted background helped the illusion; but the effect of the lavish use of colour on flesh, drapery, and backgrounds cannot now be readily appreciated since so little of it has survived in more than ghostly traces.

EARLY CLASSICAL PERIOD

In the figurative arts a distinctive style developed, in some respects representing as much of a contrast with what came afterward as with what went before. Its name—Severe style—is in part an indication that the "prettiness" of Archaic art, with its patterns of drapery and its decisive action, has been replaced by calm and balance. This new tone is evident in the composition of scenes and in details such as drapery, where the fussy pleats of the Archaic chiton give place to the heavy, straight fall of an outer robe called the *peplos*. The finest artists transformed the verve of the late Archaic style into more delicate expressions of emotion, and some were clearly checking their work more deliberately against the living model.

The early Classical period saw an impressive series of sculptural works that were excellent in their own right and significant in the continuing development of technical expressive skill and naturalism such as the relief carvings of the so-called Ludovisi Throne. Moreover, for the first time individual artists—and their contributions to technical and stylistic development—can in some cases be identified through Roman copies and written descriptions.

The finest examples of early Classical architectural sculpture are the works of the Olympia Master, an unidentified artist who decorated the pediments and frieze of the Temple of Zeus at Olympia.

A metope from the Temple of Zeus at Olympia, now at the Archaeological Museum, in Olympia.

In the east pediment, which shows men and women preparing for a chariot race, his figures display the sobriety and calm characteristic of the early Classical period. The men stand in the new, relaxed pose (the weight of the body being carried mainly by one leg) that was to be used by most sculptors throughout the period; and the women wear the peplos, its broad, heavy folds lending severity to the static composition. The west pediment, with a scene of struggling men and centaurs, has something of the rigid formality of the Archaic spirit, but here—and in the metopes that show the labours of Heracles—the artist has acutely observed differences of age in the human bodies and differences of expression—pain, fear, despair, disgust—in the faces. This was something new in Greek sculpture and, in fact, cannot be readily matched in other works of this period.

In freestanding sculpture—at this time, more commonly bronze than marble—the works of Myron (of Eleutherae, in Attica) were among the most celebrated of the period. Myron's most famous work is the *Discobolos* ("discus thrower"), of which a Roman copy survives. Another of Myron's works surviving in copy is a sculpture of Athena with the satyr Marsyas. The interplay of mood and action between the figures in this freestanding group is new, foreshadowed only by the now lost group of the Tyrant Slayers erected in Athens at the end of the 6th century.

Because bronze was often looted and corrodes easily, the majority of freestanding sculptures from this period have been lost. Some, however, have been rediscovered in the 20th century, the *Poseidon* and the *Charioteer* from Delphi, for instance, although they have been eclipsed in fame by the Riace bronzes, a remarkable pair of warriors dredged from the sea in 1972. The finer of these latter bronzes, although it probably represents a mortal, has a supernatural glamour and a ferocity quite unlike the calm solemnity conventionally admired in Classical works. This derives partly from the glowing

The famous *Charioteer* from the sanctuary of Apollo at Delphi, now in that town's Archaeological Museum.

surface of the swelling musculature and the use of inlay for eyes, teeth, and lips.

HIGH CLASSICAL PERIOD

Since Roman times, Greek art of the second half of the 5th century BCE has been generally regarded as the high point in the development of the Classical tradition. It was the most refined expression of the Greek view of their gods as men and of their men as partaking of the divine. The aesthetic result of this concept was that the bestial or supernatural was abjured in representations of the divine; thus, even a Greek monster, such as the centaur, seems plausible as an image combining humanity and divinity. To some degree, the idealization of human figures was facilitated by the Greeks' traditional concern with proportion and pattern. As a result of the value placed on the ideal image, the representation of extremes (of age or youth, for example, or of deep emotion) and of individuality was ignored or little practiced. Even figures engaged in violent or painful action have a calm, detached expression. Another reflection of the value placed on the ideal image is an increasing preoccupation with the "heroic nude."

During the high Classical period, Athens resumed a position of importance as an artistic centre of the Greek world. Once most of the Greek homelands were secure from the Persian threat, the funds that had been provided to Athens by the Greek states to lead their defense were turned by the statesman Pericles to the embellishment of Athens itself. This task attracted sculptors, masons, and other artists to Athens from all over the Greek world. It is largely the work of these artists, under the guidance of Athenian masters, that determined what is now recognized as the high Classical style.

Of the several types of sculpture that flourished during the high Classical period, major statuary is least represented in surviving examples. Phidias, the most influential sculptor of the period, made two huge cult images plated with gold and ivory, the statue of Athena for the Parthenon and a seated statue of Zeus for the temple at Olympia that was one of the seven wonders of the ancient world. These works amazed and overawed viewers through all antiquity, but no adequate copies survive.

Another important sculptor of the period, whose work can be seen through copies, was Polyclitus, from Argos. Polyclitus embodied his views on proportion in his *Doryphoros* ("spear bearer"), called "The Canon" because of its "correct" proportions of one ideal male form.

Unlike freestanding statues, architectural sculpture from the high Classical period has survived in abundance. The Parthenon sculptures must have been executed by many different hands, but, because the overall design was by Phidias, the composition and details undoubtedly reflect his style and instructions. The pedimental figures and frieze, especially, display the Classical qualities of idealization. These allow an approximate assessment of Phidias's style and the importance of his contribution to the establishment of the Classical idiom. About the time that full employment for sculptors in Athens on the Parthenon came to an end, there began a distinguished series of carved relief gravestones for Athenian cemeteries. The general type had been familiar in Archaic Athens, and the practice continued in other parts of Greece through the early Classical period, mainly in the islands and in Boeotia. The new Attic series, with calm and dignified groups of figures in generalized settings of domesticity or leave-taking, exploited effectively the rather impersonal calm in figure and features of the Classical conventions.

The other important class of sculpture, much of which has survived in the original, is the dedicatory—votive reliefs or major works like the *Nike* ("Victory") found at Olympia, made by Paeonius. This work, and others that belong to the last years of the century, such as the frieze from the balustrade of the temple of Athena Nike on the Acropolis at Athens, gives a clear indication of progress and change in sculptural style. In the representation of the female body, true femininity was at last achieved through observation; in these works the figures are no longer like male bodies with the more obvious female characteristics added, which had generally been true of earlier works. Drapery, which had for its patterns been an important element of female figures in the Archaic period, has a heaviness, almost a life of its own in the Parthenon sculptures. In the sbalustrade, it is shown pressed tight against the body revealing the forms of the limbs and torso clearly beneath, with brittle, dramatic folds standing clear of the surface.

LATE CLASSICAL PERIOD

The 4th century saw a dramatic increase of wealth in Greece, but one concentrated on the periphery of the Greek world—with the western colonies, the eastern Greeks, and the increasingly powerful Macedonian kingdom in the north. Macedonian power, culminating in Alexander the Great's annexation of the whole Persian Empire in the 4th century, was to transform Greek art as effectively as it did Greek life and politics. Even before Alexander's accession, however, the seeds of change were sown. The many new centres and patrons for artists may have made it easier for them to break with Classical conventions established in 5th-century Athens or by dominant 5th-century artists like Polyclitus. The trend was toward greater individuality of expression, of emotion, and of identity, leading eventually to true portraiture. The last was encouraged by the ambitions and pride of rulers such as the Macedonian kings or by the royal houses of Hellenized provinces in the western Persian Empire. To the same sources can be traced the new interest in monumental tomb construction. Men were aspiring more openly to divinity, and Greek art was no barrier to its explicit expression. It is clear, however, that artists were conscious of the values that were set in the 5th century, and by no means did they act as revolutionaries in styles or techniques. The development of Greek art was swift but smooth, and personalities lent impetus to the development rather than changing its flow dramatically.

Three names dominate 4th-century sculpture, Praxiteles, Scopas, and Lysippus. Each can be appreciated only through ancient descriptions and copies, but each clearly contributed to the rapid transition in sculpture from Classical idealism to Hellenistic realism. Praxiteles, an Athenian, demonstrated a total command of technique and anatomy in a series of sinuously relaxed figures that, for the first time in Greek sculpture, fully exploited the sensual possibilities of carved marble. His

Aphrodite (several copies are known), made for the east Greek town of Cnidus, was totally naked, a novelty in Greek art, and its erotic appeal was famous in antiquity. The *Hermes Carrying the Infant Dionysus* at Olympia, which may be an original from his hand, gives an idea of how effectively a master could make flesh of marble.

The reputation of Scopas, from the island of Paros, came from the intensity of expression with which he imbued his figures. Fragments of his work at Tegea show his technique in the deep-sunk eye sockets that characterize his faces and that transform the hitherto passionless features of Classical sculpture into studies of intense emotion.

Lysippus, from Sicyon in the northern Peloponnese, was Alexander's favourite sculptor. He was true to the Classical tradition in demonstrating his views on proportion by sculpting athlete figures in different poses, although his types have heavier bodies and smaller heads than those of the Classical standard set down by Polyclitus. But he adds something to these single figure studies; for the first time they are composed in such a way that the viewer is invited to move around them, and they are not tied to a single optimum viewpoint, as even Praxiteles' figures had been.

Another innovation, in the development of which Lysippus must also have played a part, is portraiture; he carved likenesses of Alexander. Nevertheless, portraits of contemporaries were still exceptional, and many early portraits are semi-idealized studies of the great philosophers, statesmen, or poets of the Classical period. And yet, it is clear that by now the use of live models was commonplace, as can be judged from the works or copies that survive and from stories of Praxiteles' use of his mistress Phryne as a model or of Lysippus's brother taking casts from life.

HELLENISTIC PERIOD

Styles of Hellenistic sculpture were determined by places and schools rather than by great names. Pergamene sculpture is exemplified by the great reliefs from the altar of Zeus, now in Berlin, and copies of dedicatory statues showing defeated Gauls. These, like the well-known *Nike of Samothrace*, are masterful displays of vigorous action and emotion—triumph, fury, despair— and the effect is achieved by exaggeration of anatomical detail and features and by a shrewd use of the rendering of hair and drapery to heighten the mood.

The *Laocoön* group, a famous sculpture of the Trojan priest and his two sons struggling with a huge serpent, probably made by Rhodian artists in the 1st century CE but derived from examples of suffering figures carved in the 1st century BCE, is a good example of this applied to a freestanding group.

In vivid contrast, a fully sensual treatment of the female nude was achieved by careful surface working of the marble, and the accentuation of femininity by the incorporation of sloping shoulders, tiny breasts, and high full hips. It is the Hellenistic Aphrodite, such as the *Venus de Milo*, who proliferates in Roman copies. The sculptural groups such as *Laocoön* were novel, demanding a palatial or sanctuary setting and far removed from earlier two-figure groups or the more nearly comparable but one-view pedimental compositions. The new realism extended to the portrayal of old age, decrepitude, disease, low life, and even the grotesque. Alexandria, in its major and minor (clay) works of sculpture, seems to have been one of the important schools in this genre. For the first time in Greek art, babies were rendered as other than reduced adults. In portraiture, the idealizing tendencies of the 4th century were still strong, and portraits of kings or poets were overlaid by conceptions of kingship or artistry. It was to take Roman patronage to enforce a more brutal realism in portraiture of contemporaries.

Two of the most significant developments in Hellenistic sculpture had nothing to do with the evolution of new styles or types of compositions. The first was the production of accurate copies of earlier works, which began by about 100 BCE, in part occasioned by the demand from the Roman West. This production stimulated interest in the styles of the great Classical sculptors and helped to determine the decidedly Classical atmosphere of early imperial art. The second, related development is the creation of original works deliberately in the style of the late Archaic, early Classical, or full Classical periods. This archaizing can be seen as both a reaction against the more exuberant Hellenistic sculptural styles and a response to the new interest in the Classical past.

CHAPTER TWO

ROMAN SCULPTURE

There are many ways in which the term "ancient Roman art" can be defined, but it is generally used to describe what was produced throughout the part of the world ruled or dominated by Rome until around 500 CE, including Jewish and Christian work that is similar in style to the pagan work of the same period.

The Romans were always conscious of the superiority of the artistic traditions of their neighbours. Such works of art as were made in or imported into Rome during the periods of the monarchy and the early republic were produced almost certainly by Greek and Hellenized Etruscan artists or by their imitators from the cities of central Latium; and throughout the later republican and the imperial epochs many of the leading artists, architects, and craftsmen had Greek names and were Greek-speaking.

According to tradition, the earliest image of a god made in Rome dated from the 6th century BCE period of Etruscan domination and was the work of Vulca of Veii. A magnificent terra-cotta statue of Apollo found at Veii may give some notion of its character. In the 5th, 4th, and 3rd centuries BCE, when Etruscan influence on Rome was declining and Rome's dominion was spreading through the Italian peninsula, contacts with Greek art were no longer chiefly mediated via Etruria but, instead, were made directly through Campania and Magna Graecia; "idealizing" statues of gods and worthies mentioned in literature as executed in the capital during this period were clearly the works of visiting or immigrant Greek artists. The plundering of Syracuse and Tarentum at the end of the 3rd century BCE marked the beginning of a flow of Greek art treasures into Rome that continued for several centuries and played a leading role in the aesthetic education of the citizens.

The first appearance of three art forms that expressed the Roman spirit most eloquently in sculpture can be traced to the Hellenistic Age. These forms are realistic portraiture showing a preference for the ordinary over the heroic or legendary, in which every line, crease, wrinkle, and even blemish was ruthlessly recorded; a continuous style in narrative art of all types; and a three-dimensional rendering of atmosphere, depth, and perspective in relief work and painting.

LATE REPUBLIC

Ancestral *imagines*, or funerary masks, made of wax or terra-cotta, had become extremely individualized and realistic by the middle of the 2nd century BCE. The source of this realism is in the impact on Rome of late-Hellenistic iconography; although this use of masks was rooted in ancient Roman social and religious practice, there is no basis for a belief that the Romans and Etruscans had, from early times, been in the habit of producing death masks proper, cast directly from the features of the dead. It was undoubtedly their funerary customs that predisposed the Romans to a taste for portraits; but it was not until around 100 BCE that realistic portraiture, as an art in its own right, appeared in Rome as a sudden flowering, and to that time belong the beginnings of the highly realistic heads, busts, and statues of contemporary Romans—in marble, stone, or bronze—that have actually survived. Coin portraits of public personages, whose names and dates are recorded, greatly assist in determining a chronological sequence of the large-scale likenesses, the earliest of which can be attributed to the period of Sulla (82–79 BCE). The style reached its climax in a stark, dry, linear iconographic manner that prevailed around 75–65 BCE and that expressed to perfection current notions of traditional Roman virtues; of this manner, a marble head of an elderly veiled man in the Vatican is an outstanding illustration.

Shortly thereafter, an admiration for earlier phases of Greek art came into fashion in the West, and verism was toned down at the higher social levels by a revival of mid-Hellenistic pathos and even by a classicizing trend that was to stamp itself upon Augustan portraits.

Meantime, in sepulchral custom, the ancestral bust had become an alternative to the ancestral mask, a development exemplified in a marble statue of a man wearing a toga and carrying two such busts in the Capitoline Museums at Rome. Portrait busts and figures carved on numerous stone and marble grave stelae (slabs or pillars used for commemorative purposes), characteristic of the

The Capitoline Museums' statue of a patrician with the busts of his ancestors is life-sized.

late republican epoch, suggest the persistence of a preference for severe pose in middle-class and humbler circles. There are some 1st-century-BCE portraits that suggest that the making of death masks proper (arguably a sophisticated idea) was occasionally practiced at this time.

There are no narrative reliefs from Rome that can confidently be assigned to a date before 100 BCE. The only definitely dated 2nd-century-BCE relief depicting an episode from contemporary Roman history, a frieze with the Battle of Pydna on Lucius Aemilius Paulus's victory monument at Delphi, was worked in 168 BCE in Greece. The most familiar republican example of this form of art as practiced in the West is frieze decoration from the so-called Altar of Ahenobarbus. In these, prosaic documentation of Roman census procedure is juxtaposed with depictions of Greek sea nymphs, a conjunction of literalism and borrowed poetry typical of subsequent Roman art.

Funerary narrative sculpture of the late republic is exemplified in a monument of the Julii, at Saint-Rémy (Glanum), France. The base of this structure carries four great reliefs with battle and hunt scenes that allude not only to the mundane prowess of the family but also to the otherworldly victory of the souls of the departed over death and evil, since figures of the deceased, accompanied by personifications of death and victory, merge into one of the battle scenes.

AUGUSTAN AGE

The hallmark of portraits of Augustus is a naturalistic classicism. The rendering of his features and the forking of his hair above the brow is individual. But the Emperor is consistently idealized and never shown as elderly or aging. A marble statue from Livia's Villa at Prima Porta, which presents him as addressing, as it were, the whole empire, is the work of a fine Greek artist who, while adopting the pose and proportions of a classical Hellenic statue, perfectly understood how to adopt these to the image that Augustus cultivated as emperor. On his ornate cuirass (armour protecting the chest and back), Augustus's aims and achievements are recorded symbolically in a series of figure groups. A marble portrait statue found on the Via Labicana represents the Emperor as heavily draped and veiled during the act of sacrificing as *pontifex maximus* ("chief priest"); and a bronze head from Meroe, in Sudan, the work of a Greco-Egyptian portraitist, depicts him as a Hellenistic king. Of the female portraits of the period, one of the most charming is a green basalt head of the Emperor's sister, Octavia, with the hair dressed in a puff above the brow and gathered into a bun behind—a popular coiffure in early Augustan times.

In many respects, the noblest of all Roman public monuments that were adorned with sculpture is the Ara Pacis Augustae ("Augustus's

Altar of Peace"), founded in 13 BCE and dedicated four years later. It stood in the Campus Martius and has been restored not far from its original site. On its reliefs—of Luna marble, a white marble quarried in Italy and not, as had earlier been the case, imported from Greece—it set a standard of distinction surpassed by no later work, with the harmonious blending of contemporary history, legend, and

Ara Pacis, detail of the procession dedicating the same. The dedication, on January 30, 9 BCE, was recorded in Ovid's *Fasti* as well as in Augustus's own *Res Gestae Divi Augusti.*

personification, of figure scenes and decorative floral motifs. The altar proper was contained within a walled enclosure, with entrances on east and west. On the upper part of the external faces of the south and north precinct walls ran a frieze representing the actual procession (of Augustus, members of his family, officers, priests, magistrates, and the Roman people) to the altar's chosen site on its foundation day (July 4, 13 BCE). Flanking the western entrance were depictions of Augustus's prototype Aeneas sacrificing on his homecoming to the promised land of Italy, and, art historians speculate, the suckling of Romulus and Remus by the she-wolf. The eastern entrance was flanked by personifications of Roma and of Mother Earth with children on her knees flanked by figures symbolizing air and water. On the exterior of the walls, beneath all these figure scenes, was a magnificent dado filled with a naturalistic pattern of acanthus, vine, and ivy, perhaps a translation into marble of a gorgeous carpet or tapestry used in the ceremony. Swags of fruit and flowers that decked the interior faces of the precinct walls may represent real swags that were hung on the temporary wooden altar erected for the foundation sacrifice. The procession was continued in a much smaller frieze on the inner altar, from which figures of Vestal Virgins and of sacrificial victims and their attendants have been preserved. Delightful studies of children and such homely incidents as conversations between persons taking part in the procession introduce an element of intimacy, informality, and even humour into this solemn act of public worship. The style of the altar's floral decoration strongly suggests that the sculptors who carved it were Greeks from Pergamum.

JULIO-CLAUDIAN AND FLAVIAN PERIODS

The imperial portraiture of Tiberius and Caligula was generally precise but academic work, but some of the female court portraits reflect not only the fashions for elegant simplicity and extreme elaboration in female coiffure but also a subtle poetry. Two possible extremes of tone are clearly marked by the contrasting busts of Claudius and Nero, the former uncomfortably uncompromising, the latter flatteringly Hellenic.

In the Emperor Vespasian's portraits, something of the old, dry style returned. This can be observed in his striking likeness on one of two historical reliefs that were unearthed in Rome near the Palazzo della Cancelleria. A similarly sketchy and impressionistic handling of the hair is found on the emperor Titus's portraits, whereas the third Flavian emperor, Domitian, affected a more pictorial hairdo in imitation of the coiffure introduced by Nero. Still more picturesque are the female hairstyles of the time, which display piles of corkscrew ringlets or tight, round curls. The Cancelleria reliefs date from the close of Domitian's reign and depict, respectively, Vespasian's triumphal entry and reception in Rome in 70 CE and Domitian's *profectio* ("setting out"), under the aegis of Mars, Minerva, and Virtus, for one of his northern wars. They are worked in a two-dimensional, academic, classicizing style that is in marked contrast with the vivid, three-dimensional rendering of space and depth, with brilliant interplay of light and shade, on the panels of the Arch of Titus in the Roman Forum. The latter reliefs, which present two excerpts from Titus's triumph in Palestine, were carved in the early 80s. The late Domitianic classicizing manner appears again in the frieze of the Forum Transitorium, which the emperor Nerva completed. This conflict of relief styles within the Flavian period is but one illustration of the ceaseless, unpredictable ebb and flow of different aesthetic principles throughout the history of imperial art.

AGE OF TRAJAN

In portraits of Trajan, a deepening of the bust, which was already seen in the later Flavian period, was carried a stage further; there is a new fluidity in the molding of the face; in the hair, which is plastered down across the brow, there is a partial revival of the late republican linear style.

Aesthetically, one of the finest known likenesses of the Emperor is a marble head from Ostia. On his monumental column there is a series of less idealized and probably more faithful renderings of his features. The coiffures of Trajanic ladies are, if anything, even more elaborate and extravagant than those of their Flavian predecessors.

The reliefs of Trajan's Column, illustrating the two Dacian campaigns of 101–102 and 105–106 and winding up the shaft in a spiral band of Parian marble, are generally recognized to be the classic example of the continuous method of narration in Roman art. The episodes merge into one another without any punctuation, apart from an occasional tree; Trajan appears again and again in different situations, activities, and costumes.

Including its pedestal, Trajan's Column measures 125 feet (38 m) high.

A statuesque figure of Victory separates the histories of the two wars. There are 23 spirals and about 2,500 figures. A high level of technical accomplishment is maintained throughout, and the interest and excitement of the theme never flag. Since the figures of men and animals had to be distinguished from a distance, they are inevitably overlarge in proportion to their landscape and architectural settings; and in order to avoid awkward empty spaces along the upper edges of the band and to preserve an allover, even, tapestrylike effect, background figures in the scenes are reared in bird's-eye-view perspective above the heads of those in the foreground. These carvings were once brightly painted, with weapons and horse trappings added in metal.

The column (the interior of which contains a spiral staircase) had first been intended primarily as a lookout post for viewing Trajan's architectural achievements—his forum and its adjacent markets. By the time of its dedication in 113, when the relief bands had been added and an eagle planned for the top of the capital, it had become a war memorial.

To the last years of Trajan's reign or to the early years of that of his successor should be attributed four horizontal panels that adorn the main passageway and the attic ends of the Arch of Constantine in Rome. If fitted together they would form a continuous frieze of three main scenes, which are, from left to right, an imperial triumphal entry, a battle, and the presentation to the Emperor of prisoners and the severed heads of captives by Roman soldiers. It seems clear that these sculptures were made between around 115 and 120, perhaps for the Temple of Divus Trajanus and Diva Plotina that was erected by Hadrian just to the north of the column. The presence on this frieze of chain-mail corselets, rarely seen on Trajan's Column, seems to indicate that that type of armour first came into general use in late Trajanic or early Hadrianic times. These reliefs do not depict realistic fighting, as do those of the column, but a kind of ideal or dramatized warfare, with the Emperor himself participating in the melee and the soldiers wearing plumed and richly embossed parade helmets; the scenes melt into one another with total disregard of spatial and temporal logic.

A third example of Trajanic monumental sculpture is the relief decoration of the Arch of Trajan at Beneventum (Benevento), which is covered with pictorial slabs, the subjects of which are arranged to carry out a carefully balanced and nicely calculated order of ideas. Those on the side facing the city and on one wall of the passageway present themes from Trajan's policy and work for Rome and Italy; those on the side toward the country and on the other wall of the passageway allude to his achievements abroad. With two exceptions, where a pair of scenes forms a single picture, each panel is a self-contained unit. The reliefs already show something of the classicizing, two-dimensional character of Hadrianic work. Indeed, it seems likely that, although the arch itself was either decreed or dedicated in 114 or 115, some of the panels in which Hadrian is given a peculiar prominence were not carved until the early years of the latter's principate.

AGE OF HADRIAN

In the iconography of the age of Hadrian, certain Hellenizing features—the wearing of a short Greek beard by the males and the adoption by the females of a simple, classicizing coiffure—are harmonized with new experiments. The depth of the bust increases, there is greater plasticity in the modelling of the face, the men's curly hair and beards are pictorially treated, and the irises and pupils of the eyes are marked in. Many marble portraits of the Emperor survive from all over the empire, but of his likenesses in bronze only one is extant—a colossal head recovered from the Thames River in London, torn from a statue erected in the Roman city and probably the work of a good Gaulish sculptor. Portrait statues of Hadrian's Bithynian favourite, Antinoüs, reveal a conscious return in the pose and proportions of the body to Classical Greek standards, combined with a new emotionalism and sensuousness in the rendering of the head.

The most interesting and perhaps the earliest of the monumental reliefs of Hadrian's day are two horizontal slabs once exposed in the Roman Forum. Both carry on one side similar figures of victims for the Suovetaurilia sacrifice and on the other side different historical scenes: in the one case, Hadrian doling out the *alimenta* ("poor relief") to Roman citizens, in the presence of a statuary group of Trajan and Italia with children; in the other case, the burning of debt registers. At one end of each of these scenes is carved a figure, on a base, of the legendary Greek musician Marsyas, whose statue in the Forum may once have been in part enclosed by the panels. In the background of both historical pictures are carved in low relief various buildings in the Roman Forum that can be identified. The two scenes display the characteristically Hadrianic two-dimensional style, as do three large panels, with the Emperor's head restored and depicting an imperial triumphal entry, an *adlocutio*, and an *apotheosis*, respectively. Eight medallions gracing the Arch of Constantine give pleasantly composed and lively, if Hellenizing, pictures of sacrifice and hunting. Some of them depict Antinoüs accompanying the Emperor, whose portraits have been recut as likenesses of Constantine the Great and of his colleague Licinius.

Interment began to supersede cremation as a method of disposing of the dead during the second quarter of the 2nd century, and

Hadrian's reign saw the beginnings of a long line of carved sarcophagi that constituted the most significant class of minor sculptures down to the close of the ancient Greco-Roman world.

ANTONINE AND SEVERAN PERIODS

Portraits of Antonine imperial persons, of which a bronze equestrian figure of Marcus Aurelius on the Capitol and a great marble bust of Commodus as Hercules in the Palazzo dei Conservatori are perhaps the most arresting examples, display a treatment of hair and beard, deeply undercut and drilled, that grew ever more pictorial and baroque as the 2nd century advanced. This produced an impression of nervous restlessness that contrasts with the still, satin smoothness of the facial surfaces, particularly in the iconography of Commodus. To all this picturesqueness, Septimius Severus added yet another ornamental touch—the dangling, corkscrew forelocks of his patron deity, Sarapis. The female hairstyles of the time are characterized first by a coronal of plaits on top (Faustina the Elder), next by rippling side waves and a small, neat bun at the nape of the neck (Faustina the Younger, Lucilla), and then by stiff, artificial, "permanent" waving at the sides and a flat, spreading "pad" of hair behind (Crispina, Julia Domna).

Of the state reliefs of this epoch, the earliest are on the base of a lost column set up in honour of Antoninus Pius and Faustina the Elder. The front bears a dignified, classicizing scene of apotheosis: a powerfully built winged figure lifts the Emperor and Empress aloft, while two personifications, Roma and Campus Martius, witness their departure. On each side is a *decursio*, or military parade, in which the riders farthest from the spectator appear not behind the foot soldiers but high above their heads—a remarkable instance of the bird's-eye-view perspective carried to its logical conclusions. All the figures in these side scenes are disposed on projecting ledges, a device employed again about 20 years later on Marcus Aurelius's column. Eleven rectangular sculptured panels—similar to those on the Arch of Trajan at Beneventum but displaying greater crowding of figures, livelier movement, and a pronounced effect of atmosphere and depth—depict official occasions and ceremonies in the career of Marcus. The contrast in style between the spiral reliefs of the Column of Marcus Aurelius, put up under Commodus and depicting Marcus Aurelius's northern campaigns, with those of its Trajanic predecessor, is a measure of the change of mood that the Roman world experienced during the course of the 2nd century. The diminished proportions of the squat, doll-like figures, their herding together in closely packed, undifferentiated masses, their angular, agitated gestures, and the stress laid throughout on the horror and tragedy of war suggest that the empire is facing an unknown future with diminished security and that man is at the mercy of some unaccountable power, the supreme embodiment of which is an awe-inspiring winged, dripping figure, personifying the rainstorm that saved the Roman army from perishing from thirst. Again, in the imperial *adlocutiones* that punctuate this frieze, where the Emperor stands in a strictly frontal pose high above the heads of his audiences, can be seen a remarkable return to the conventions employed in primitive art for expressing the concept of the ruler as transcendental being.

The spirit of the times is reflected no less vividly in carved sarcophagi. Their themes—familiar myths, battles, hunts, marriages, and so on—allude allegorically to death and the destiny of the soul thereafter. The classicizing, statuesque tradition is also maintained in late 2nd- and early 3rd-century columned sarcophagi, originating in the workshops of Asia Minor but freely imported into, and sometimes imitated in, Rome and Italy. On such pieces single figures or small groups of figures occupy niches between colonnettes. Among the most impressive examples is a great sarcophagus at Melfi, in Puglia, Italy, with a couch-shaped lid, on which the figure of a girl lies prostrate in the sleep of death.

3RD AND 4TH CENTURIES

A new tension between naturalism and schematization marks the history of late-antique portraiture. In likenesses of Alexander Severus, the facial planes are simplified, and the tumbling curls of the 2nd-century baroque have been banished in favour of a skullcap treatment of the hair and sheathlike rendering of the beard. Toward the middle of the 3rd century, under Philip the Arabian and Decius, this clipped technique in hair and beard was combined with a return to something of the old, ruthless realism in the depiction of facial furrows, creases, and wrinkles. For a time, Gallienus reinstated the baroque curls and emotional expression, but in the later decades of the century the schematic handling of hair, beards, and features reappeared.

Finally, in the clean-shaven faces of Constantine the Great and his successors of the 4th and early 5th centuries, the conception of a portrait as an architectonic structure came to stay, and the naturalistic, representational art of the Greco-Roman world was exchanged for a hieratic, transcendental style that was the hallmark of Byzantine and medieval iconography. The hair is combed forward on the brow in rigid, striated locks, and the eyes are unnaturally enlarged and isolated from the other features. The face is so formalized that the identification of any given portrait becomes a problem. A colossal bronze emperor (near the church of S. Sepolcro, Barletta), for example, has been given the names of several different rulers of the late 4th and early 5th centuries.

MINOR FORMS OF SCULPTURE

Of the minor forms of sculpture, none is more attractive than the art of modelling—in relief or in the round—in fine, white stucco. Decorative stucco work was cheaper and easier to produce than carving in stone or marble. Soft and delicate in texture, it was equally elegant whether left white or gaily painted. In domestic architecture it was a useful alternative or accessory to painting; notable are such examples as a pure white, exquisite vault decoration showing ritual scenes with small-scale figures, from a late republican or early imperial house near the Villa Farnesina in Trastevere; handsome pairs of large white griffins, framed in acanthus scrolls against a vivid red ground, in the late republican House of the Griffins on the Palatine; and a frieze depicting the story of the *Iliad*, in white figures on a bright blue background, in the House of the Cryptoporticus, or Homeric house, at Pompeii. For the use of this technique in palaces, the figure work in Domitian's villa at Castel Gandolfo in the Alban hills can be cited; it can be found in such public buildings as the Stabian and Forum baths and the Temple of Isis at Pompeii. The loveliest and most extensive stucco relief work in a semiprivate shrine is that in the underground basilica near the Porta Maggiore, Rome, where the scenes all allude to the world beyond the grave, to the soul's journey to it, and to the soul's preparation for it in this life. Some of the best surviving stuccos are in tombs: the tomb of the Innocentii and the tomb of the Axe under the church of S. Sebastiano on the Via Appia; the tombs of the Valerii and the Pancratii on the Via Latina; and the tomb of the Valerii under St. Peter's, Rome, where the interior walls of both the main and subsidiary chambers are almost completely covered with recesses, niches, and lunettes (semicircular or crescent-shaped spaces) containing stucco figures.

Ivory was another popular material for minor sculpture. It was worked in the round, in relief, and in such forms as small portraits, figurines, caskets, and furniture ornaments. The consular and other diptychs comprise one of the most distinctive types of ivory relief work in the 4th and 5th centuries. Among them are masterpieces that kept alive the traditions of Hellenistic carving, such as a diptych of the Symmachi and Nicomachi families and some outstandingly fine examples of late antique portraiture, such as the Probus diptych at Aosta with a double portrait of Honorius, the Felix diptych (dated 428), and one of Boethius, consul in 487. Fine examples of wood carving are panels with biblical scenes on the 5th-century door of the church of Sta. Sabina on the Aventine.

Many types of carving in precious stones were practiced by Roman-age craftsmen, and it is to them that the credit goes for the majority of intaglios that have survived from ancient times. (Intaglios are engraved or incised figures depressed below the surface of the stone so that an impression from the design yields an image in relief.) The widespread taste for them is reflected in the many existing glass-paste imitations reproducing their subjects, which include portraits of both imperial and private persons, and a large variety of divine and mythological groups and figures, personifications, animals, etc.

The most impressive series of Roman gems consists of cameos representing imperial persons. These are miniature reliefs cut in precious stones with different coloured strata (so that the relief is of a different colour from the ground). Among the earliest surviving examples of the great imperial cameos are the Blacas onyx (portraying Augustus in the guise of Jupiter), the *Gemma Augustea* (a sardonyx, or an onyx with parallel layers of sard), the *Grand Camée de France* (a sardonyx, probably carved under Caligula), and a sardonyx cameo of Claudius with Jupiter's aegis. Late antique examples of the craft are a rectangular sardonyx portraying Constantine the Great and members of his house and an onyx with busts of Honorius and Maria.

Closely akin to cameos and vessels cut in precious stones are their substitutes in opaque "cameo glass," worked in two layers, with the designs standing out in white against a dark-blue or bright-blue background. To this

The *Gemma Augustea* is now in the Kunsthistorisches Museum, in Vienna. It shows Augustus seated next to the goddess Roma, with both figures trampling the armour of defeated enemies.

class belong a blue vase from Pompeii, with Cupids gathering grapes; the Auldjo vase, with an exquisitely naturalistic vine; and the celebrated Portland vase, the scenes on which have always been the subject of scholarly controversy but are generally supposed to depict myths relating to the afterlife.

EARLY CHRISTIAN SCULPTURE

Truly Christian art—that is, with a style quite distinctive from Pagan Roman art— did not exist before the end of the 2nd or beginning of the 3rd century. Its style evolved from the current Greco-Roman art. The new elements lay not in form but in content: places of worship very different from pagan temples, iconography drawn from the Scriptures. As the hold of the church over public and private life grew, these new elements tended to set traditional subjects completely aside. Early Christian art, while deeply rooted in Greco-Roman art, became a new entity, as distinct from ancient art as from that of the Middle Ages. An obvious difference is the absence of monumental public sculpture. Early Christian sculpture was limited to small pieces and private memorials and

ROME AND CONSTANTINOPLE

The new capital at Constantinople (ancient Byzantium), founded by the emperor Constantine the Great (306–337), became an important centre of art. The art produced there, now known as Byzantine art, extended throughout the entire Christian East. It is customary to distinguish early Christian art of the West or Latin part from the Christian art of regions dominated by the Greek language and to consider the latter proto-Byzantine, while acknowledging, however, a certain latitude in the initial date of this separation: 330, the foundation of Constantinople; 395, the separation of the Greek part of the empire from its Latin sector; or, finally, the reign of Justinian (527–565).

only gradually became incorporated into ecclesiastical architecture.

The imagery of sarcophagi followed an evolution similar to that of the catacomb paintings. Biblical subjects were introduced into pagan or neutral compositions. The oldest Christian sarcophagi, from the second or third quarter of the 3rd century, were hardly distinguishable from pagan sarcophagi. On one at Sta. Maria Antiqua, Rome, a seated philosopher reading a scroll, a praying figure, and a "Good Shepherd" are "Christianized" by the scenes that accompany them on either side: Jonah resting and the Baptism of Christ.

During the 4th century this iconography was enriched and became more strictly narrative; the miracles of Christ, fully described, were included, the crossing of the Red Sea was often depicted in a long frieze, and the episodes of the Passion of Christ—his arrest, his trial before the Jewish council, his presentation to Pilate, and the Way of the Cross—often extended along the faces of the sarcophagi. The Crucifixion itself was represented by only a bare cross, surmounted by a crown enclosing the monogram of Christ: thus, the symbolic image of the triumph over death. This hesitation to portray the dead Christ on the Cross, an ignominious mode of punishment reserved by the Romans for slaves and abject criminals, disappeared only gradually during the course of the 5th and 6th centuries.

CHAPTER THREE

SCULPTURE OF THE MIDDLE AGES

J ust as early Christian art is divided between the East and West, so, too, is the art of the Middle Ages. In the West the end of Early Christian art is easier to determine. Closely tied to Roman art, it finished with the collapse of the empire at the end of the 5th century. Then, transformed into a multitude of regional art styles, it assimilated various influences from the East and from the barbaric peoples who superseded their Roman masters.

The Byzantine era began with the transference of the capital of the Roman Empire from Rome to the site of ancient Byzantium on the Bosporus in the year 330 CE, the new capital thereafter being called Constantinople, after its founder, the emperor Constantine I. Constantine had 17 years earlier been responsible for recognizing Christianity, and from the outset he made it the official religion of the new city. The art dedicated to the service of the faith, which had already begun to develop in the days when Christians were oppressed, received official recognition in the new centre and was also subjected to a number of new influences, so that it owed a debt on the one hand to Italy and Rome and on the other to Syria and Asia Minor, where Oriental elements were prominent.

BYZANTINE SCULPTURE

Sculpture underwent changes similar to those in architecture. The decorative work in Hagia Sophia, a 6th-century cathedral in Constantinople, illustrates its nature. In the Classical world naturalistic representation had prevailed; at Hagia Sophia the forms are still basically representational, but they are treated in an abstract manner. Capitals of the period are similarly stylized even when they use bird or animal forms, for these are usually treated as part of an overall balanced pattern. With this tendency toward stylization in architectural sculpture, it is not surprising to find that three-dimensional, representational sculpture was progressively going out of fashion. Portrait sculptures had been made of most of the early emperors, and the texts report that a mounted figure of Justinian I topped a column in front of Hagia Sophia, but that was the last of the series. Figural compositions in high relief had adorned sarcophagi and similar reliefs had found a place on the walls of churches, but virtually none of these dates from later than Justinian's reign. Instead, flat slabs with low-relief ornament akin to that on the capitals and cornices of Hagia Sophia, some of it even purely geometric, came into vogue. These slabs were used for the lower sections of windows or to form a screen between the body of the church and the sanctuary; they were later to develop into the high structures called iconostases, which eventually became universal in Orthodox churches.

IVORIES

The minor sculptural arts are essential to any treatment of medieval sculpture in general, partly because some of the most able masters of the period preferred to work on small-scale objects and patronage was ready to support them. Most important are the ivories. They comprise a wide variety of types, ranging from small pyxides—circular vessels used in the liturgy—to large-scale works made up of a number of separate panels, like the famous throne of Maximian, the Archbishop of Ravenna, at Ravenna. Most usual, however, were the flat plaques used as diptychs, book covers, etc. Considerable numbers of these, dating mostly from the late 5th and early 6th centuries, have been preserved. After about the middle of the 6th century, however, ivories become rarer: very few can be dated to the period between the reign of Justinian and the revival of Byzantine art in the 9th century.

Diptychs, or two-panel ivories, seem to have been popular both for use as book covers and for ceremonial purposes. The most impressive of them were imperial. In these each leaf was made up of five panels; on the central one was a portrait of the emperor; at the sides were standing figures of the consuls; below were scenes, usually of tribute bearers; and above were angels upholding a bust of Christ. They thus illustrated the Byzantine ideas of hierarchy, Christ above and the world below, dominated by the emperor as Christ's vice-regent. The finest of them, known as the Barberini ivory, probably depicts Anastasius I (491–518); another, of his wife, the empress Ariadne, is divided between several collections.

More numerous today are the diptychs that were issued by the consuls on coming to office. Their fabrication ceased when the office of consul was abolished by Justinian in 541; though by no means are all the consuls portrayed before that time, leaves of the diptychs issued by a large number of them survive. Each leaf consisted of a single plaque. The earlier ones, like that of Probus (408), are still Roman in style; but those dating from just before and just after 500, which constitute the majority, are in a different style, either more ornate or very much simpler. The more elaborate ones are well rep-

Ivory diptych showing paired images of the consul Flavius Anastasius with circus scenes below (c. 517), now in the Bibliothèque Nationale, in Paris.

resented by leaves of the consul Flavius Anastasius (517); they show the consul enthroned, with lively circus scenes below. The plainer type is represented by a consular diptych of Justinian dated 521 (six years before his accession as emperor), where the decoration is confined to rosettes at the four corners and a medallion with a Latin inscription at the centre.

Most of the official ivories were probably carved at Constantinople, but it seems likely that others, which were intended for more general use or for the church, may well have been done elsewhere. Rome, Milan, Alexandria, and Antioch in Syria were all important centres, and there has been a good deal of dispute among experts as to where many of the ivories were made. Maximian's throne, the most elaborate of them all, has been assigned to Alexandria, Constantinople, and even to Ravenna itself; and there has been argument as to whether the consular diptychs were carved at Constantinople, Rome, or Alexandria.

Though caskets were no doubt often carved by the same people who carved the plaques, they constitute an independent group not only because of their form but also because they are nearly all adorned with secular motifs that have been drawn from Classical literature. The panels bearing the scenes are framed in bands adorned with rosettes or sometimes human heads in profile; because of this, the caskets are often termed "rosette caskets." The most exquisite in execution, if also mannered in style, is one known as the Veroli casket. A few caskets of different type are also known; one at Florence has the rosette borders, but they frame panels bearing Christ, the Virgin, and saints; one at Troyes, France, has no rosette borders, while its side panels show horsemen of Persian type and, at the ends, phoenixes that are distinctly Chinese. During the later part of the 12th century, soapstone plaques became more common than ivories, probably for economic reasons, but they bore low-relief decorations in a very similar style.

SCULPTURE OF THE CHRISTIAN EAST

Only after Justinian's reign did many Eastern regions submit to the ascendancy of the art of Constantinople, following until the 6th and even the 7th century the paths traced by Christian art in its beginnings. Thereafter, several regions developed their own artistic traditions, related to that of Byzantine art, but still distinguishable from the art created in the central cities of the empire.

ARMENIA

The stone construction of Armenian churches lent itself to carved decorations, and architectural sculpture was more extensively used in Armenia than in any other country of the Middle East, except Georgia. The reliefs of the 4th-century hypogeum (a subterranean structure hewn out of rock) at Aghts along with those on numerous funerary stelae antedating the Arab conquest exemplify the early stages of stone sculpture. Beginning with the 6th century, and perhaps even earlier, floral and geometric motifs as well as figure representations were carved around the windows of the churches, between the arches of the blind arcades, and on the lintels and the lunettes over the doors. Decorative ornaments became increasingly intricate during the later periods.

The outstanding example in Armenian art of the use of architectural sculpture is the Church of the Holy Cross, built in the early 10th century on the island of Aghthamar in Lake Van; this is the earliest medieval example, either in the East or in the West, of a stone building entirely covered with relief sculpture. Around the dome and on the four facades may be seen a variety of animals, vine and other floral scrolls, and large figures of saints and scenes from the Hebrew Bible. A portrait of King Gagik I Artsruni, offering to Christ a model of the church he had erected, appears on the west facade. Such donor portraits, sometimes carved in the round as at Ani, were one of the characteristic features of the decoration of Armenian churches.

GEORGIA

A distinct Georgian sculptural tradition did not emerge until the advent of Christianity, which stimulated a demand for a large number of carved stone reliefs. The earliest of these were based on Early Christian models. In the 8th and 9th centuries the high-relief figures of Early Christian art gave way to figures rendered in wholly linear fashion. In the 10th and 11th centuries the reliefs became gradually more plastic and expressive until they were again freed, to a considerable degree, from the background. At the same time there was an increasing interest in the disposition of figures in a harmonious design. By the 12th century, however, sculptors were beginning to look more to ornamentation than to figural representation. Repetition of themes characterized most of Georgian sculpture in subsequent centuries. Sculpture of all periods was always smaller than life-size.

COPTIC EGYPT

Strictly speaking, the adjective Coptic, when it is applied to art, should be confined to the Christian art of Egypt from the time when the Christian faith may be recognized as the established religion of the country among both the Greek-speaking and Egyptian-speaking elements of the population. In this sense Coptic art is essentially that reflected in the stone reliefs, wood carvings, and wall paintings of the monasteries of Egypt, the earliest foundations of which date from the 4th and 5th centuries CE. It is, however, common practice to include within Coptic art forms of artistic expression that have no religious intent or purpose. The term has also been used to denote stylistic characteristics dating back to the 2nd and 3rd centuries CE and perhaps earlier.

A specifically Christian art was slow in developing: when it did emerge, it was not the product of a school of Christian artists inventing new forms of expression. It continued the style current in the country, evolving from the late antique art of Egypt, in which themes derived from Hellenistic and Roman art may or may not have been given new allegorical significance. There is little direct legacy from the art of pharaonic Egypt. The most obvious survival in Christian iconography is the peculiar looped form of cross derived from the ancient Egyptian writing of the word for life (*ankh*). Less convincing is the connection postulated between the concept of *Maria lactans* (representations of the Virgin nursing her child) and bronze and terra-cotta statues of the ancient Egyptian goddess Isis suckling the infant sun god Horus or between representations of saints on horseback and some late figures of the adult Horus in an identical pose.

The extent to which Egypt exerted a creative influence on Christian art is uncertain in the absence of material remains of the Christian period from Alexandria, the great metropolis of Egypt from the time and a city that played an important a role in the intellectual life of the early church. A series of Christian ivory carvings, of unrecorded provenance, is frequently referred to as Alexandrian on stylistic considerations and adduced as proof of a continuing artistic skill in the Hellenistic tradition.

Objects found in the hinterland depart from the Classical canons of proportion and mode of representation. Political and economic conditions in Egypt from the time of its incorporation in the Roman and, later, Byzantine empires doubtless account for much of the provincial appearance of Egyptian and Coptic art and the emergence of a freer, more popular folk style. Lack of the kind of patronage that had been given by the pharaohs, Ptolemies, and, to some extent, Roman emperors to the old religion of Egypt meant an impoverishment of schools of skilled craftsmen, avoidance of costlier materials, and a decline in the high standard of finish. Particularly noticeable is the absence of carving in the round, of work of monumental scale, and of the use of the harder ornamental stones that had been characteristic of pharaonic art.

Characteristic Coptic stylistic features are to be observed in tombstones from the Delta site of Terenuthis. These depict the dead man frontally posed beneath a gabled pediment of mixed architectural style, hands extended at right angles from the body and bent upward from the elbow in the *orans* (praying) position, a pose that appeared frequently in the earliest Christian art in Rome. There is no firm evidence, however, that the community was Christian. Similarly, the series of architectural elements carved in relief from Oxyrhynchus and Heracleopolis may not all be from Christian buildings. The earlier material from Heracleopolis, dating probably from the 4th century, is notable for its figure subjects drawn from classical mythology, carved in a deep relief that leaves them almost freestanding, producing an effective play of light and shade. As such reliefs were painted, the absence of fine detail in the carving was less noticeable.

Much of the material available for a study of Coptic sculpture has not been found in context, and, in the absence of assured information concerning its provenance and of circumstantial evidence for dating, it is impossible to provide a detailed account of the development of Coptic sculpture. In general, the figures are stiff in pose and movement; there is a tendency for the carving to become flat, and there is little in the way of narrative scenes drawn from biblical stories. The most successful carvings are probably the impressive variety of decorated capitals, particularly from the monasteries of Apa Jeremias at Ṣaqqārah and of Apa Apollo at Bāwiṭ. Among them are basket-shaped examples decorated with plaitwork, vine and acanthus leaves, and animal heads. The form imitates a style introduced into Constantinople by the emperor Justinian I, and it is clear that, in the hinterland of Egypt, there was during the 6th century certain artistic influence on Coptic art from Byzantium, despite religious and political differences.

WESTERN CHRISTIAN SCULPTURE

With the dissolution of the Roman Empire in the West, cultural hegemony passed to the Eastern Empire, but older traditions remained in western Europe and intermingled with several invaders—Germanic tribes arriving from the north and Christians arriving from Constantinople as well as from Rome. The Merovingian art of the Franks, which was culturally predominant throughout Europe in the 6th century, survives principally in grave relics, such as jewelry, hollowware, and the like.

In Italy the Lombards, who invaded the country in 568, propagated Germanic art, but there is a strong Mediterranean influence in the sculpture—stone plaques for choir screens, altars and altar canopies, sarcophagi, and details of architecture, for example; the abstract decorations, many of them interlaced motifs, were to be blended with more and more Byzantine elements. The creatures and vegetation become almost impossible to recognize—they aspire, as it were, to be ornamental stone writing rather than representation. Similar ornaments were also applied in stucco; for example, in S. Salvatore at Brescia and especially in the famous Tempietto at Cividale del Friuli (both 8th century). At Cividale del Friuli, standing figures of saints have been incorporated in decoration in which the Byzantine influence is obvious.

In Ireland, monumental crosses represented the Celtic Christian tradition, and similar Anglo-Saxon crosses may be found in England. The abstracted decoration recalls the relief style in Italy, but here the surface is not a flat plane but is packed with round, knoblike projections that create a plastic rather than a glyphic effect.

CAROLINGIAN AND OTTONIAN PERIODS

The cultural revival of the Carolingian period (768 to the late 9th century), stimulated by the *academia palatina* at Charlemagne's court, is the first phase of the pre-Romanesque culture, a phase in which late Classical and Byzantine elements amalgamated with ornamental designs brought from the East by the Germanic tribes. The German Ottonian and early Salian emperors (950–1050), who succeeded the Carolingians as rulers of the Holy Roman Empire, assumed initially the Carolingian artistic heritage, although Ottonian art later evolved into a distinct style.

Little Carolingian sculpture has survived, but in Ottonian days the sculpting of freestanding statues was taken up again, although the earliest specimens, serving as reliquaries, were closely related to the silversmith's and goldsmith's art; for example, the famous statue of Sainte-Foy at Conques (France) and the *Golden Madonna* at Essen. The reliefs on the wooden doors of Sankt Maria im Kapitol at Cologne display an affinity with the mid-11th-century Romanesque ivories of the Meuse district. The Carolingian bronze doors in Aachen were imitated at Mainz, where Bishop Willigis had similar portal wings made for his cathedral. He was far surpassed, however, by Bernward at Hildesheim, who had the still extant door wings of the cathedral (1015) decorated with typological images in parallel, scenes from the Hebrew Bible and the New Testament; in theme, the images go back to early Christian examples Bernward had seen in Italy, but the force of the gestures and the use of unadorned surface as dramatic interval in the episode of Adam and Eve reproached by the Lord has no precedent in the history of art. The influence of Classical art manifests itself clearly in the so-called Christ's Column (c. 1020; St. Michael's, Hildesheim), which, with its figures spiralling around the shaft, reminds one of the triumphal columns of Trajan and Marcus Aurelius.

ROMANESQUE

The term "Romanesque"—coined in 1818— denotes in art the medieval synthesis of the widespread Roman architectural and artistic heritage and various regional influences, such as Teutonic, Scandinavian, Byzantine, and Muslim. Although derived primarily from the remains of a highly centralized imperial culture, the Romanesque flowered during a period of fragmented and unstable governments. It was the medieval monasteries, virtual islands of civilization scattered about the continent, which provided the impetus—and the patronage—for a major cultural revival.

The bronze Christ's Column is a modest prophecy of the monumental spirit that would distinguish the sculptural decoration of the new monastic buildings rising in much of western Europe. Developed in the abbey doorways and on the pillars and capitals of cloisters, where the sculptor had to learn anew the technique of stone carving and of rendering the human figure, this spirit gradually grew stronger.

During the 11th century more and more churches were constructed in the Romanesque style, the massive forms of which are another indication of this sculptural instinct. Romanesque sculpture culminated in France in the great semicircular relief compositions over church portals, called tympanums. The example of the abbey church at Moissac (c. 1120–30), which represents the Apocalyptic vision with the 24 elders, is a particularly brilliant demonstration of how devices of style can so transform the objects of nature that they seem entirely purged of terrestriality. All the forms are suspended in a predominating plane that denies physical space. Differences in scale are masterfully exploited: the tiny figures of the elders are a foil to the looming image of Christ in the centre. With great consistency, every detail has been subjected to a process of stylization that produces rhythmic patterns in the drapery, hair, and feathers. The central figure is so flattened as to appear disembodied, whereas the two towering angels have been so attenuated that their bodies have lost all mass.

The astonishing variety that master sculptors such as Gislebertus, Benedetto Antelami, and Nicola Pisano achieved within the confining principles of Romanesque style can be illustrated, on the one hand, by the tympanums of the cathedrals of Burgundy, such as the spectral *Last Judgment* at Autun or the *Pentecost* at Vézelay, and, on the other, by the less visionary sculpture of Provence, such as that of the church of Saint-Trophime in Arles or of the church in Saint-Gilles, which retain many of the forms and characteristics of Classical antiquity.

Another sculptural form that reappeared in Europe during the latter part of the Romanesque period was sepulchral sculpture, in which a sculptured figure of the deceased was cut or molded on top of a sarcophagus or on the sepulchral slab set into the floor of an abbey or cloister.

The west tympanum of the Cathedral of Saint-Lazare, in Autun, depicts the Last Judgment. Noted for its expressionistic carving and technical proficiency, it was carved by Gislebertus before 1135.

EARLY GOTHIC

Throughout this period, as in the Romanesque period, the best sculptors were extensively employed on architectural decoration. The most important agglomerations of figure work to survive are on portals, and, in this, the church of Villard de Honnecourt assumes great significance. The western portals (built 1137–40), part of a total facade design, combined features that remained common throughout the Gothic period: a carved tympanum (the space within an arch and above a lintel or a subordinate arch); carved surrounding figures set in the *voussoirs*, or wedge-shaped pieces, of the arch; and more carved figures attached to the sides of the portal.

If one compares the portals of the west front of Chartres Cathedral (c. 1140–50) with those of early 13th-century Reims, one can see that the general direction of the changes in this early period of Gothic sculpture was toward increased realism. The movement toward realism is not manifest in a continuous evolution, however, but in a series of stylistic fashions, each starting from different artistic premises and achieving sometimes a greater degree of realism but sometimes merely a different sort of realism. The first of these fashions can be seen in the sculpture on the west front of Chartres Cathedral. That the Christ and the Apostle figures are in some sense more human than the Romanesque apparitions at Vézelay and Autun (c. 1130) need hardly be argued. That the figures, with their stylized gestures and minutely pleated garments, are at all "real" is doubtful. That their forms are closely locked to the architectural composition is clear. The features of the Chartres sculpture had a wide distribution; they are found, for example, at Angers, Le Mans, Bourges, and Senlis Cathedrals. There are stylistic connections with Burgundy and also with Provence. The fashion lasted from c. 1140 to 1180.

The centre of development for the second style lay in the region of the Meuse. The activity of one of the chief artists, a goldsmith called Nicholas of Verdun, extends at least from the so-called Klosterneuburg altar (1181) into the early years of the 13th century. His style is characterized by graceful, curving figures and soft, looping drapery worked in a series of ridges and troughs. From these troughs is derived the commonly used German term for this style—*Muldenstil*. This drapery convention is essentially a Greek invention of the 4th century BCE. It seems likely that Nicholas seized the whole figure style as a tool to be used in the general exploration of new forms of realism. It remained extremely popular well into the 13th century. A rather restrained version of the style decorated the main portals of the transepts (the transversal part of a cruciform

Statues of Saint Simeon and John the Baptist, from the west facade of Reims Cathedral. Reims was the site of 25 coronations of the kings of France.

church set between the nave and the apse or choir) of Chartres (c. 1200–10). It is also found in the earliest sculpture (c. 1212–25) of Reims Cathedral and in the drawings of the sketchbook of French architect Villard de Honnecourt (c. 1220).

In the opening years of the 13th century yet another type of realism emerged. It seems to have originated at Notre-Dame, Paris (c. 1200), and to have been based on Byzantine prototypes, probably of the 10th century. The looping drapery and curving figures were abandoned; instead, the figures have a square, upright appearance and are extremely restrained in their gestures. Figures in this style are found at Reims, but the major monument is the west front (c. 1220–30) of Amiens Cathedral.

Once again, the style changed. On the west front of Reims worked a man called after his most famous figure, the Joseph Master. Working in a style that probably originated in Paris c. 1230, he ignored the restraint of Amiens and the drapery convolutions of the *Muldenstil* and produced (c. 1240) figures possessing many of the characteristics retained by sculpture for the next 150 years: dainty poses and faces and rather thick drapery hanging in long V-shaped folds that envelop and mask the figure.

Another aspect of this quest for realism was the spasmodic fashion throughout the 13th century for realistic architectural foliage decoration. This resulted in some astonishingly good botanical studies—at Reims Cathedral, for example.

The effects elsewhere in Europe of this intense period of French experiment were piecemeal and disjointed. In England, the concept of the Great Portal, with its carved tympanum, voussoirs, and side figures, was virtually ignored. The remains of a portal the style of which may be connected with Sens Cathedral survive from St. Mary's Abbey, York, England (c. 1210). Rochester Cathedral (c. 1150) has carved side figures, and Lincoln Cathedral (c. 1140) once had them. The major displays of English early Gothic sculpture, however, took quite a different form. The chief surviving monument is the west front of Wells Cathedral (c. 1225–40), where the sculpture, while comparing reasonably well in style with near-contemporary French developments, is spread across the upper facade and hardly related at all to the portal.

In Germany, the story is similar. On the border between France and Germany stands Strasbourg, the cathedral of which contains on its south front some of the finest sculpture of the period (c. 1230). It has an emotional character, common in German art, that represents an effort to involve and move the spectator. That emotionalism is again found at Magdeburg Cathedral in a series of *Wise and Foolish Virgins* (c. 1245) left over from some

The *Bamberg Horseman* (c. 1230–35) adorns the interior of Bamberg Cathedral, in Bamberg, Germany. It may depict Stephen I, the first king of Hungary, who was canonized in 1083.

abandoned sculptural scheme. Influenced by Reims rather than Chartres, the sculpture of Bamberg Cathedral (c. 1230–35) is a heavier version of the *Muldenstil* than that at Strasbourg.

In the west choir (c. 1250) of Naumburg Cathedral, the desire for dramatic tension is exploited to good effect, since the figures—a series of lay founders in contemporary costume—are given a realistic place in the architecture, alongside a triforium gallery. Naumburg also has a notable amount of extremely realistic foliage carving.

It is hard to say what a French mason would have made of this English and German work. With the major Spanish work of the period, however, he would have felt instantly at home. Burgos Cathedral has a portal (1230s) that is very close to the general style of Amiens, and its layout is also, by French standards, reasonably conventional.

HIGH GOTHIC

Late sculptural developments of the early Gothic period were of great importance for the High Gothic period. The Joseph Master at Reims and the Master of the Vierge Dorée at Amiens both adopted a drapery style that, in various forms, became extremely common for the next century or more; both introduced into their figures a sort of mannered daintiness that became popular. These features appear in an exaggerated form in some of the sculpture for the Sainte-Chapelle ("Holy Chapel"), Paris.

The field of sculpture that expanded with great rapidity in this period was the private one, represented by tombs and other monuments. For this, the family feeling of Louis IX was partly responsible. By making sure that both his remote ancestors and his next of kin got a decent burial—or reburial—he was responsible for an impressive series of monuments (the remnants of which are now chiefly in Saint-Denis) executed mainly in the years following 1260. Louis IX had a large share in popularizing the idea of the dynastic mausoleum, and many other important people followed suit.

Louis's masons popularized two important ideas. One was the tomb chest decorated with small figures in niches—figures generally known as weepers, since they often represented members of the family who might be presumed to be in mourning. Later, in the early 14th century, the first representations appear of the heavily cloaked and cowled professional mourners who were normally employed to follow the coffin in a funeral procession. The second innovation introduced by Louis's masons lay in the emphasis given to the effigy. Around 1260 the first attempts were made to endow the effigy with a particular character. This may not have involved portraiture, but it did involve a study of different types of physiognomy, just as the botanical carving of the early Gothic period had involved a study of different kinds of leaves.

A somewhat similar story may be told of English sculpture during this period. The architectural carving found at Westminster Abbey (mainly of the 1250s) has much of the daintiness of contemporary French work, although the drapery is still more like that of the early Chartres or Wells sculpture. The baggy fold forms of the Joseph Master rarely appear in England before the sculptured angels of the Lincoln Angel Choir (after 1256).

First-rate masons continued to work on architectural sculpture in England until the end of the 13th century. Around 1295 one can still find a work such as the botanical carving of Southwell Chapter House. Even in the 14th century, there are such architectural and sculptural curiosities as the west front of Exeter Cathedral. Sculptural interest, however, in buildings such as Gloucester Cathedral Choir (begun soon after 1330), where the effect depends on traceried panels, is virtually nonexistent.

As in France, much of the virtuosity in carving went into private tombs and monuments. The best surviving medieval mausoleum is Westminster Abbey, where a large number of monuments in a variety of mediums (especially purbeck, bronze, alabaster, and freestone) is further enhanced by some of the floors and tombs executed by Italian mosaic workers introduced by Henry III. Especially well preserved is the tomb of Edmund Crouchback, earl of Lancaster (died 1296), which has a splendid canopy and retains some of its original colouring.

As in the early Gothic period, the west of England produced some highly original work that appears to stand outside the normal canon of European development. An early example is the tomb of Edward II (c. 1330–35), which has one of the most elaborate surviving medieval canopies. It is preceded stylistically by the wooden canopies of stalls in Exeter Cathedral and thus is likely to be a translation into stone of carpenters' work.

German High Gothic sculpture is represented by dainty, elegant figures, enveloped in curving and bulky drapery, around the choir of Cologne Cathedral (consecrated in 1322). There is also some impressive figure sculpture on the west front of Strasbourg Cathedral (begun after 1277). It is strongly influenced by the Joseph Master of Reims but also by the earlier Gothic sculpture of Strasbourg itself. Although it varies in style, much of it is far more expressive than the related French work. The sculptors seem to have been trying to capture an emotive mood.

Spanish High Gothic architectural sculpture is, by French standards, more conventional than the German. Major portals exist at León (13th century) and Toledo (14th century) Cathedrals, which conform more or less to the rather elegant and mannered French style. Spain also possesses a considerable number of interesting tombs from this period.

ITALIAN GOTHIC

The figurative arts in Italy during the period 1250–1350 have a strong line of development. The most important 13th-century sculptors were Nicola Pisano and his son Giovanni. Both worked mainly in Tuscany. Nicola's style, as seen in the Pisa Baptistery (1259–60) and Siena Cathedral (1265–68) pulpits, was heavily influenced by Classical sculpture—especially by the facial types and methods of constructing pictorial relief compositions. Nevertheless, his reliefs resemble 13th-century sculpture, particularly in the handling of the drapery. In moving from Pisa to Siena, one is conscious of a transition from a strongly antique style to something closer to northern Gothic sculpture. Nicola's use of Classical ideas was linked with a search for a more realistic style. It forms, in this respect, an interesting parallel to the *Muldenstil* work of Nicholas of Verdun, who was active in the Mosan region from the late 12th to the early 13th century.

The sculptural style of Giovanni does not develop from that of his father. His pulpit in S. Andrea Pistoia (completed 1301), for instance, is technically less detailed and refined but emotionally much more dramatic. While it is possible that the emotionalism of his work was inspired by Hellenistic sculpture, it is also possible that Giovanni had travelled in and been influenced by the north, especially Germany.

Giovanni's first major independent work was a facade for Siena Cathedral (c. 1285–95).

Marble pulpit in the Church of San Andrea, in Pistoia, Italy. It is the work of Giovanni Pisano, who continuously reintegrated the antique style into more northerly and contemporary Gothic forms.

The lower half alone was completed, and it survives in the present building along with a large proportion of Giovanni's imposing figure sculpture.

The fame of Nicola's workshop spread to other areas of Italy. For S. Domenico in Bologna, his workshop made a shrine for the body of St. Dominic (1260s). In Milan, a shrine for the body of St. Peter Martyr was made (1335–39) by Giovanni di Balduccio in a style derived from the Pisano workshop. The most famous Pisano "exports," however, were Arnolfo di Cambio, who worked for the papal court in Rome, and Tino di Camaino, who worked at the Neapolitan court.

Although Arnolfo worked alongside Giovanni Pisano during the 1260s, their works have little in common. Arnolfo's sculpture is very solid and impassive. He excelled at formal, static compositions, such as were required for church furniture and for tombs. He designed the funerary chapel as well as the tomb of Pope Boniface VIII and like the Pisanos was architect as well as sculptor.

Tino di Camaino went south after training in Siena and a successful career in Tuscany. Sometimes his style approaches the elegance and sweetness of northern 14th-century sculpture, but there is generally a residual heaviness, especially in the faces, that reminds one of his origins in the Pisano circle. He was famous as a tomb sculptor, and the largest collection of his monuments is in Naples (much of the sculpture, however, was executed by his workshop).

The workshop of the facade of Orvieto Cathedral and the work of the sculptor and architect Andrea Pisano (no relation to Nicola and Giovanni) are less clearly connected with the Pisano tradition. Andrea Pisano is known chiefly through the bronze doors completed for the Baptistery of Florence Cathedral during the 1330s. The scenes of the life of St. John the Baptist are set in *quatrefoils* (a four-lobed foliation), a common High Gothic decorative motif. Within this awkward shape, the episodes are composed with masterly skill.

Andrea had a son, Nino Pisano, about whom little is known but from whose hand a group of Madonnas survives. They are interesting in that they veer strongly in the direction of daintiness and sweetness and, to this extent, look more northern than almost any other group of Italian sculpture before the early work of Lorenzo Ghiberti.

INTERNATIONAL GOTHIC

The plastic arts are harder to understand in this period, because so much has been destroyed. For example, enormous quantities of goldsmiths' work owned by the French royal family have vanished. A few of the remaining pieces testify to the quality of the work, which is beautifully finished and gaily coloured in the technique of *en ronde bosse* enameling.

More seriously, large quantities of private monumental sculpture have been lost in France and the Low Countries. The main sculptor of the French royal family in the second half of the 14th century was André Beauneveu. His reputation was so widespread that he earned a mention by Jean Froissart, the medieval poet and court historian whose *Chronicles* of the 14th century remain the most important and detailed document of feudal times in Europe and the best contemporary exposition of chivalric and courtly ideals. Beauneveu produced a large number of monuments, especially for King Charles V, of which several effigies survive.

Claus Sluter worked for Charles V's brother Philip the Bold, duke of Burgundy. Sluter's surviving work is mainly at Dijon, France, where he was active from about 1390 to about 1406. His figure style is very strongly characterized and detailed and, at times, emotional. This suggests that his origins are German and that he may have come from the region of Westphalia. The intrusive realism of Sluter's work, however, is also symptomatic of a gradual change in sculptural style during this period. The strong characterization of the faces of his figures finds parallels in the near-contemporary triforium busts and Přemyslid tombs in St. Vitus's Cathedral in Prague. Sluter's drapery style, which veers dramatically away from the somewhat reticent elegance of previous court sculpture, also has parallels in the east. Bohemia and Austria possess a series of Madonna figures (*Schöne Madonnen*) swathed in extremely elaborate and artificial drapery arrangements.

England stands apart from much of the development represented by Sluter's style. The royal tombs in Westminster Abbey, which extend up to Richard II (died 1400), do not reflect changes subsequent to the phase of Beauneveu. Further, a fashion for bronze effigies, going back to the effigy of Henry III (1291–93), persisted in England.

LATE GOTHIC

In the years around 1400, when International Gothic flourished, Italian and northern artists had achieved some sort of rapprochement. Under the renewed influence of antique art, Italy drew away again, and it was not until the 16th century that the north showed any real disposition to follow suit in the imitation of Classical models. Sculptural development in the 15th century is harder to trace—partly because much crucial work (especially in the Low Countries) has been destroyed. It is clear, however, that elaboration rather than restraint was the rule—indeed, the exceptions to the rule (mainly found in France) stand out. A taste for the highly complicated and

INTERNATIONAL SCULPTORS

In the late Gothic period, the amount of art produced by foreign artists for countries such as Hungary, Poland, and Scotland increased. Competition between countries for the work of the best artists was not new. Throughout the Middle Ages artists travelled widely. In the 13th century Villard de Honnecourt went from northern France to Hungary, and Roman marble workers journeyed to Westminster. In the period c. 1400 there was much interchange between northern and southern Europe. In the 15th century, this general pattern was confirmed; the Netherlandish sculptor Gerhaert Nikolaus von Leyden, for instance, became court sculptor in Vienna, and the Italian sculptor and architect Andrea Sansovino served the Portuguese court in the 1490s. There is also the work of the Franconian sculptor Veit Stoss for the Polish court at Cracow (c. 1480) and the work of Bernt Notke of Lübeck for Aarhus (Denmark), Tallinn (Estonia), and Stockholm (c. 1470-90). An altar executed by Meister Francke of Hamburg for Helsingfors (1420s) and Hugo van der Goes's panels for the Palace of Holyrood, near Edinburgh (1470s) are further examples.

elaborate persisted, especially in Spain and Germany. Like painters, sculptors enjoyed giving extremely realistic detail and expression to their figures. Like architects, they enjoyed complicated tracery work, often encasing their compositions in tabernacle-like enclosures of brilliantly fantastic architecture.

In Germany, two of the more important sculptors were Gerhaert Nikolaus von Leyden and Michael Pacher of Brunico. They were followed by a number of virtuoso southern German artists: Veit Stoss of Nürnberg, Tilman Riemenschneider of Würzburg, and Adam Kraft of Nürnberg. In northern Germany, the most original figure was Bernt Notke of Lübeck. Much of the fantastic decorative involvement of his work may now seem overwhelming. The love of realistic detail is well illustrated by Notke's monumental group of St. George and the Dragon at St. Nicholas's Church in Stockholm, where the dragon's spines are made from real antlers. The group as a whole is, of course, of wood, a medium that could be employed to create intricate, open, thin, and spiky forms impossible in stone.

On the whole, the sculpture produced in France seems to show more decorative restraint. Certainly, the chief French works surviving take the form of large groups, as in the Tonnerre *Entombment* (1450s), or of architectural schemes in which the decoration is clearly subordinate to the figures, as in Châteaudun, Castle Chapel (c. 1425).

Restraint is also notable in the chantry chapel of Richard Beauchamp, earl of Warwick (c. 1450; Warwick), which has some obvious motifs taken over from the workshop of Sluter. But many of the chantry chapels so common in 15th-century England show an extraordinary mixture of sculpture and tracery work more reminiscent, as an expression of taste, of Germany or Spain.

Spanish 15th-century sculpture also tended to be extremely ornate. A number of huge, carved high altarpieces survive—for instance, in the cathedrals of Burgos (1486–88) and Toledo (begun 1498). Some of the altarpieces, like that at Toledo, were designed and executed under the direction of German or Netherlandish artists.

The change from late Gothic to Renaissance was superficially far less cataclysmic than the change from Romanesque to Gothic. In the figurative arts, it was not the great shift from symbolism to realistic representation but a change from one sort of realism to another. The history of the northern artistic Renaissance is in part the story of the process by which artists gradually realized that Classicism represented another canon of taste and treated it accordingly.

But it is possible to suggest a more

profound character to the change. Late Gothic has a peculiar aura of finality about it. From about 1470 to 1520, one gets the impression that the combination of decorative richness and realistic detail was being worked virtually to death. Classical antiquity at least provided an alternative form of art. It is arguable that change would have come in the north anyway and that adoption of Renaissance forms was a matter of coincidence and convenience. They were there at hand, for experiment.

CHAPTER FOUR

RENAISSANCE AND BAROQUE SCULPTURE

The Renaissance (literally "rebirth") was the period in European civilization immediately following the Middle Ages and conventionally held to have been characterized by a surge of interest in Classical learning and values. It was in art that the spirit of the Renaissance achieved its sharpest formulation. Art came to be seen as a branch of knowledge, valuable in its own right and capable of providing man with images of God and his creations as well as with insights into man's position in the universe.

The Renaissance was followed by the Baroque period, an era in the history of the Western arts roughly coinciding with the 17th century. Its earliest manifestations, which occurred in Italy, date from the latter decades of the 16th century, while in some regions, notably Germany and colonial South America, certain of its culminating achievements did not occur until the 18th century. The work that distinguishes the Baroque period is stylistically complex. In general, however, the desire to evoke emotional states by appealing to the senses, often in dramatic ways, underlies its manifestations. Some of the qualities most frequently associated with the Baroque are grandeur, sensuous richness, drama, vitality, movement, tension, emotional exuberance, and a tendency to blur distinctions between the various arts.

EARLY RENAISSANCE

The revival of Classical learning in Italy, which was a marked feature of Italian culture during the 15th century, was paralleled by an equal passion for the beauty of Classical design in all the artistic fields; and when this eager delight in the then fresh and sensuous graciousness that is the mark of much Classical work—to the Italians of that time, seemingly the expression of a golden age—became universal, complete domination of the Classical ideal in art was inevitable.

This turning to Classical models was less sudden and revolutionary than it seemed. Throughout the history of Romanesque and Gothic Italian art, the tradition of Classical structure and ornament remained alive; again and again, in the 12th and 13th centuries Classical forms—the acanthus leaf, moulding ornaments, the treatment of drapery in a relief—are imitated, often with crudeness, to be sure, but with a basic sympathy for the old imperial Roman methods of design. Nicola Pisano, at work in the mid-13th century, was but the first of many Italian artists, particularly sculptors, to turn definitely to Roman antecedents for inspiration.

Sculpture was the first of the arts in Florence to develop the Renaissance style. Some would date the beginning of the Renaissance to the sculptural competition in 1401 for the bronze doors of the Baptistery of the cathedral of Florence; others would propose the commission to Donatello and Nanni di Banco in 1408 for four seated saints for the facade of the cathedral. The competition reliefs for the bronze doors, submitted in 1402, reveal a change in attitude toward sculpture, and the figures of the Evangelists are the manifestation of that change. The development of Florentine sculpture roughly parallels the development in painting from a dignified monumental style to a relaxed sweetness, although there is no one in painting to approach the rich inventive genius of Donatello.

Donatello was one of the most outstandingly original artists in Western history. He undoubtedly was influenced by the concepts of antiquity current in Florence, but there was relatively little antique sculpture visible for him to study in his formative years. He first appears as a mature genius working on two of the major

projects of the 15th century, the sculptural decoration of the cathedral of Florence and of the
guild church of Orsanmichele.

His *St. George*, begun c. 1415 for the
niche of the Armourer's Guild at Orsanmichele,
indicates the new direction in sculpture. Here
he reveals such a deep knowledge of the
human figure at rest and in movement that
he may already have begun his investigation
into proportion and the statics and dynamics
of the human figure. But the tension between
repose and action—the representation,
in fact, of pause—also is a psychological
achievement, hardly to be matched in
earlier sculpture. It is noteworthy, too, that the
monumental simplicity and power of the piece
is achieved by such a subtle manipulation of
the planes and such a technical virtuosity in
carving the marble that the observer is rarely
concerned with the material. The figure is
neither flesh nor stone; it simply is.

In the relief under the niche occupied
by *St. George*, Donatello introduced another
great innovation that was to have unlimited
repercussions in Florentine art. Relief has
always been a problem for sculptors because
it must follow a narrow path between the
two-dimensionality of painting and the three-
dimensionality of full-round sculpture. Donatello
conceived of a very low relief in which the
subtle modelling of planes suggests the illusion
of depth and figures moving in space while

still respecting the integrity of the plane. He continued to develop the potentialities of this relief style throughout his long career and strongly determined the kind of relief sculpture executed in Florence.

In his brief career Nanni di Banco was as prolific and inventive as Donatello. In his earliest works, such as the *Isaiah*, he approached more closely the Classic ideal than did Donatello, and in his late work at the Porta della Mandorla he began to evolve a relaxed style that was to have its greatest impact after mid-century. About 1411–13 he executed the *Quattro Santi Coronati* ("Four Crowned Saints") for the niche of the woodworkers and stoneworkers guild at Orsanmichele. In this commission he solved one of the most difficult problems facing the sculptor, that of the group conceived in the round. Although some of the figures still retain certain Gothicizing elements in the draperies and in the heads, the major impression is of a group of Roman senators born again in the Renaissance. The group is bound together by the spatial relation of one to the other and by a kind of mute conversation in which they are all engaged.

Lorenzo Ghiberti won the competition for the bronze doors of the Baptistery. He began work in 1403 and set the doors in place in 1424. Ghiberti's fame rests upon his second set of doors, the *Gates of Paradise* (1425–52). The gilded bronze reliefs are treated almost like paintings, for they are rectangular in format and

Panel depicting the biblical story of Cain and Abel from Ghiberti's *Gates of Paradise*. The panel simultaneously depicts several separate events from the story.

contained within a frame. Unlike the earlier doors, in which the ground plane is simply a neutral backdrop, it is here treated in such a way that it suggests sky and space. Figures are placed in landscape or in perspectivally rendered architecture to suggest a greater depth to the relief than actually exists. At the time that he was executing his first set of bronze doors, Ghiberti undertook to cast the first life-sized bronze statue since antiquity, his *St. John the Baptist* (1412–16) for Orsanmichele. Although the figure and its draperies reveal Ghiberti's strong adherence to a late Gothic style, with this work he moved technically into the Renaissance. The influence of Donatello and Nanni di Banco liberates the *St. Matthew* (1419–22) at Orsanmichele from the older traditions. Ghiberti achieved fame in his own time as a bronze founder and as the master of the shop in which many sculptors and painters of the early Renaissance were trained.

Jacopo della Quercia was the most important sculptor of 15th-century Siena. He executed the Fonte Gaia (1414–19), a public fountain for the Piazza del Campo, the main square of Siena, and was awarded the commission for a baptismal font in the baptistery of Siena Cathedral. Always a procrastinating artist, he postponed work on the font to such a degree that the reliefs were finally awarded to other sculptors, including Donatello and Ghiberti. Jacopo's major work is the relief sculpture around the main portal of S. Petronio, Bologna (1425–38). The sculptural treatment of the low relief figures and the suggestion of a space adequate to contain them parallels the painting of Masaccio. The dramatic vigour and powerfully conceived forms had a great influence on the young Michelangelo.

Donatello dominated Florentine sculpture of the second quarter of the 15th century. He executed a series of prophets and a *Cantoria*, or singing balcony, for the cathedral, saints for Orsanmichele, decorative reliefs and bronze doors for the Old Sacristy of S. Lorenzo, and a bronze *David* that comes closer to recapturing the spirit of antiquity than any other work of the early Renaissance—indeed, the very idea of a freestanding sculpture of a nude hero was without precedent since antiquity. During the decade 1443–53 Donatello was in Padua executing the equestrian statue of Gattamelata to stand in front of the church. Erasmo da Narni, called Gattamelata, was a *condottiere*, or leader of mercenary troops, who rose to a position of importance. The statue is an idealization of nature in both horse and rider and a reinterpretation of antiquity. Donatello certainly knew the antique statue of Marcus Aurelius in Rome during his stay there (1431–33). He uses the concept of antiquity, the pose of the antique bronze horses at St. Mark's in Venice, and the forms of the war-horse of his own time. The rider is

Donatello's *Gattamelata*, in front of the Basilica of Sant'Antonio, in Padua. The statue established a prototype for equestrian monuments in the West.

clothed in quasi-antique armour and bears little or no resemblance to the effigy on Gattamelata's tomb inside the church. Donatello is not concerned with particulars but with the idealized and generalized aspects of man that reveal his potential nobility. The *Gattamelata* states the basic concept that almost all equestrian statues have followed since that time. Donatello's presence in Padua gave rise to a productive local school of bronze sculptors and workers, and his reliefs on the high altar there influenced painters and sculptors of northern Italy.

One of his first works upon his return to Florence was a wooden statue of Mary Magdalene for the baptistery of the cathedral. The nervous energy and conscious distortion of forms that may be detected in all his work becomes explicit in the emaciated figure clothed in her own hair. This same emotionalism and distortion is even more pronounced in his last work, the pulpits for the church of S. Lorenzo in Florence.

Antonio Pollaiuolo expresses in his sculpture the same sort of muscular activity and linear movement as in his painting—he has the energy but not the interest in emotion found in Donatello. His small bronze *Hercules and Antaeus* (c. 1475) is a forceful depiction of the struggle between these two powerful men from classical mythology. The angular contours of the limbs and the jagged voids between the figures are all directed toward expressing tautness and muscular strain, and the work is one of the earliest examples of the statuette in modern times.

In complete contrast with Pollaiuolo, Desiderio da Settignano is perhaps best known for his portraits of women and children, although he also executed two public monuments of major importance in Florence—the tomb of Carlo Marsuppini in Sta. Croce (c. 1453–55) and the *Tabernacle of the Sacrament* in S. Lorenzo (1461). The tabernacle, which was probably assembled and completed by assistants after Desiderio's death, indicates the new trends taking shape in Florentine sculpture. The central panel employs a perspectivized space. The figures moving into that space are defined in a linear manner that emphasizes contours and billowing draperies to suggest movement. The lateral, full round figures of angels are modelled with a delicacy and subtlety of surface to create relaxed and sweet figures very different from Donatello's strong, virile early saints.

Antonio Rossellino collaborated with his older brother Bernardo on the tomb of Leonardo Bruni (c. 1445–49) in Sta. Croce but soon became the dominant personality in the family business. The great sculptural complex of the Cardinal of Portugal tomb (1461–66) in S. Miniato al Monte at Florence reveals the same general tendencies as Desiderio's contemporary work. The tomb is decorated with soft and relaxed angels and a tender Madonna and Christ Child in the roundel. Similar tendencies can be found in such artists as Agostino di Duccio, Mino da Fiesole, and Luca della Robbia.

Andrea del Verrocchio was more interested than these sculptors were in movement, which he expressed in a somewhat restrained manner. His group of *Christ and St. Thomas* for Orsanmichele (c. 1467–83) solves the problem of a crowded niche by placing St. Thomas partly outside the niche and causing him to turn inward toward the figure of Christ. His large equestrian statue of Bartolomeo Colleoni (1483–88) in Venice descends from Donatello's *Gattamelata*, but a comparison of the two works reveals Verrocchio's evidence of greater interest in movement. The *Putto with Dolphin* (c. 1479) is at once an exquisite fountain decoration, an antique motif restated in Renaissance terms, and the clearest statement of Verrocchio's interest in suggested movement. The child in the piece is seen to be turning; the movement is reinforced by the fish, and the suggestion of motion culminates in the actual movement of the water spouting from the dolphin's mouth. Verrocchio also reveals his indebtedness to Desiderio in the way he treats the surfaces.

MICHELANGELO AND THE HIGH RENAISSANCE

Sixteenth-century sculpture is dominated by the figure of Michelangelo Buonarroti.

Michelangelo is said to have learned sculpture from the minor Florentine sculptor Bertoldo di Giovanni, who provided a link with the tradition of Donatello. An early work, the *Madonna of the Stairs* (c. 1492; Casa Buonarroti, Florence), reflects a type of Donatello Madonna and Donatello's very low relief. After the expulsion of the Medici from Florence, Michelangelo fled to Bologna; there he executed three figures for the tomb of S. Domenico and saw the powerful reliefs of Jacopo della Quercia. By 1496 he was in Rome, where he carved a Bacchus, now in the Bargello, Florence. Michelangelo recaptures the antique treatment of the young male figure by the soft modulation of contours. The figure seems to be slightly off-balance, and the parted lips and hazy eyes suggest that he is under the influence of wine. The little faun also joins in the Bacchic revel by slyly stealing some grapes. In his first major sculptural work, the 21-year-old artist succeeded in capturing the spirit of the antique as no artist before him had done. The *Pietà*, commissioned by a French cardinal, was begun immediately upon the completion of the *Bacchus*. The motif of the pietà is German in origin, but it is so completely transformed by Michelangelo that the work is one of the harbingers of the High Renaissance. The robes of the Madonna are exaggerated to create a solid base for the pyramidal composition. The figure of Christ is bent and twisted, in part to express the suffering of the crucifixion and in part to make it conform to the contours of the pyramid. All is directed toward creating a calm, dignified, and stable composition that expresses emotion and religious fervour by implication rather than by overstatement. The work is carried to a higher degree of finish than any of the succeeding works, and it is one of the few that Michelangelo signed.

In 1501 Michelangelo was recalled to his native city of Florence to execute an over-life-size *David*. When the piece was completed, Michelangelo's contemporaries judged it too important to place out of sight high up on the cathedral, as had been originally proposed, and a committee voted to place it in front of the Palazzo Vecchio, the seat of Florentine civic government. Michelangelo's technical virtuosity is dramatically demonstrated by the fact that he extracted a figure about 14 feet (4 metres) tall from a spoiled block. The youthful *David* was one of the symbols of Florence. Michelangelo sees him as a slightly awkward adolescent with large hands and feet, the body of a boy, and the head of a young man—a powerful figure who has not yet realized his full potential. The balance of the figure is subtly arranged to keep the bearing leg under the head while permitting the apparently nonbearing leg to be relaxed. The positions are reversed in the arms, giving the cross-axis balance of working and relaxed members. The head turns to the left to meet

Michelangelo's *David*, at the Accademia, in Florence. In 1873, the *David* was moved from the Piazza della Signoria to the Accademia to protect it from weathering and other kinds of damage.

Goliath and the stone of the sling is concealed in the right hand. It is this subtle balance and adjustment of parts to create a unified and harmonious whole that places this work firmly in the High Renaissance style that was appearing simultaneously in painting and architecture.

The Roman years (1506–16) are characterized by what Michelangelo later called the tragedy of the tomb. He had been called to Rome to execute a monumental sepulchre for Pope Julius II. The Pope's financial difficulties and the jealousies of the papal court diverted the artist from the tomb to the painting of the Sistine ceiling. The death of Julius in 1513 caused the heirs to press for a smaller tomb and rapid completion. After many years of negotiations, in 1545 a much-reduced version was set in place in S. Pietro in Vincoli, instead of in St. Peter's as originally planned. The figures by Michelangelo for the tomb are now widely scattered. Only the *Moses* remains in place from the original projects. This figure, which recalls so strongly Donatello's *St. John the Evangelist*, was intended to be placed well above the observer's head and is so adjusted. The *Dying Slave* and the *Bound Slave* are now in the Louvre. The *Victory*, also intended for the tomb, was executed c. 1532–34 in Florence, where it has remained. Four unfinished figures of slaves were carved before 1534 and remained in Florence, where they once formed part of the grotto decoration at the Pitti Palace.

With the election of Pope Leo X in 1513, Michelangelo was diverted from his projects and sent to Florence to design a facade for S. Lorenzo, a church under Medici patronage. Although Michelangelo promised that the facade would become the showplace of Italian sculpture, nothing came of the project. He was assigned instead to construct a tomb chapel as a pendant to Filippo Brunelleschi's Old Sacristy, and later to provide suitable housing for the Medici library in S. Lorenzo. While engaged in these projects Michelangelo was also put in charge of the fortifications of Florence prior to and during the siege of 1529. He complained, justly, that no one can plan and execute three projects simultaneously.

The Medici tombs (1520–34) gave the artist the opportunity to plan the architectural setting of his sculpture and to control both the light cast on the work and the position of the observer. Since the chapel was originally planned to contain the tombs of the Medici popes Leo X and Clement VII, it is best seen from behind the altar, where the papal celebrant of the mass for the dead would have stood. On the left is the tomb of Giuliano, on the right the tomb of Lorenzo, and before the observer the Madonna and Christ Child with the Medici patron saints, Cosmas and Damian;

and beneath the two sarcophagi respectively lie the recumbent figures of *Night and Day* and *Dawn and Dusk*.

The *Pietà*, or *Deposition*, in the museum of the cathedral of Florence dates from around 1550 and may have been intended by Michelangelo for use in his own tomb. The figure of Nicodemus is a self-portrait and indicates Michelangelo's deep religious convictions and his growing concern with religion. His final work, the *Rondanini Pietà* (1552–64), now in the Castello Sforzesco, Milan, is certainly his most personal and most deeply felt expression in sculpture. The artist had almost completely carved the piece when he changed his mind, returned to the block, and drastically reduced the breadth of the figures. He was working on the stone 10 days before he died, and the piece remains unfinished. In its rough state the *Rondanini Pietà* clearly shows that Michelangelo had turned from the rather muscular figure of Christ of his earlier works (as can be seen from the partially detached original right arm) to a more elongated and more dematerialized form.

MANNERISM

Whether in Rome or Florence, Michelangelo had a strong influence on sculptors of the

16th century. Vincenzo Danti followed closely in Michelangelo's footsteps. His bronze *Julius III* of 1553–56 in Perugia is derived from Michelangelo's lost bronze statue of Julius II for Bologna. Many of his figures in marble are free variations on themes by Michelangelo. In much the same way, Baccio Bandinelli attempted to rival the monumentality of Michelangelo's *David* and the complexity of his *Victory* in the statue *Hercules and Cacus* (1534), which was placed as a companion to the *David* in front of the Palazzo Vecchio. Bartolommeo Ammannati should be best known for his design of the bridge of Sta. Trinità in Florence, but his most visible work is the Neptune Fountain (1560–75) in the Piazza della Signoria, with its gigantic figure of Neptune turned toward the *David* in presumptuous rivalry.

Benvenuto Cellini through his celebrated autobiography has left a fuller account of his picturesque life than that of any other artist of the 16th century. He was in Rome from 1519 to 1540 and was one of the defenders of the pope during the siege of the Castel Sant'Angelo. In France from 1540 to 1545, he executed there the celebrated saltcellar for Francis I and the *Nymph of Fontainebleau*. The saltcellar is at once an example of 16th-century conspicuous consumption and of Mannerist conceits in art. It is of solid gold, which is covered in part by enamels as though it were a base metal. It was designed for use as a functional object upon the King's table to hold nothing more than common table salt. On his return to Florence in 1545 Cellini received the commission to cast the bronze *Perseus*. The youthful figure of Perseus seems to retain some of the airiness from his flight on the winged sandals of Hermes. He holds aloft the head of the Medusa in an outstretched arm, thus creating an open composition that exploits to the full the potential of the bronze medium. Void is almost as important as solid in this light and airy composition that would have been unthinkable and impossible in marble. Cellini intended the figure to be seen from a variety of viewing points, a relatively new idea in sculpture of this sort, and he leads the observer around by the position of the arms and the legs.

Florentine sculpture at the end of the 16th century was dominated by the Fleming Giambologna and by his shop assistants. Giambologna went to Italy for study shortly after mid-century and settled in Florence in 1557. His earlier major work in Italy is the Fountain of Neptune (1563–66) in Bologna. By early 1565 he had also cast the earliest of his many versions of the bronze *Flying Mercury* that is his most famous creation. The ideas of Cellini's *Perseus* are here carried to their logical conclusion.

Giambologna's *Hercules Fighting the Centaur Nessus* (1595–1600), in the Loggia dei Lanzi, in Florence. For three centuries Giambologna's work was more generally admired than that of any sculptor except Michelangelo.

The god borne along on the air by his winged sandals touches earth only on the slenderest base possible, which is, in fact, represented as a jet of air from the mouth of a wind god. The statue is perfectly balanced according to principles discovered early in the 15th century, yet the outthrust arms and legs give it a feeling of movement and of lightness. Giambologna understood Michelangelo's *figura serpentinata*, the upward spiralling composition, better than any sculptor of the 16th century. His marble group of the *Rape of the Sabines* (1579–83) interweaves three figures in an upward spiralling composition that prefigures the Baroque. Outside Florence, at the present Villa Demidoff in Pratolino, he carved a figure of the Apennines (1581) that seems to be a part of the living rock; it is an excellent example of late Mannerism, in which a paradoxical relationship between art and nature is often cultivated. As the favourite sculptor of the Medici, Giambologna and his prolific shop dominated Florentine sculpture at the end of the 16th century, training artists who were to carry late 16th-century ideas into the rest of Europe and prepare the way for the nascent Baroque.

In sculpture, Venice was less independent of Florence and Rome than in painting. The major 16th-century impetus came from Jacopo Sansovino, a central Italian who arrived in Venice in 1527. Sansovino never adopted the full-scale Mannerism of Florence, and his style retained a High Renaissance flavour, but his pupils Danese Cattaneo and Alessandro Vittoria were selectively able to develop the more mannered aspects of Sansovino's style into a Venetian species of Mannerism.

Vittoria's marble figures are often more directly expressive than those of Florentine sculptors. His altarpiece for S. Francesco della Vigna (1561–63) conforms with the attenuated canons of Mannerist elegance. In sculpture as in painting, the narrative Venetian style proved to be more easily adaptable to the demands of the Counter-Reformation than the abstract artiness of central Italian Mannerism.

MANNERIST SCULPTURE OUTSIDE ITALY

Both Hubert Gerhart and Adriaan de Vries, the leading exponents of northern Mannerist sculpture, can be considered as followers of the expatriate Fleming Giambologna. Gerhart worked (1583–94) at Kirchheim, Augsburg, and Amsterdam, and for the archduke Maximilian I of Bavaria, at whose court he produced bronze figures of considerable accomplishment (1598–1613). De Vries joined Rudolf's court in Prague in 1601. His *Psyche with Three Cupids* is a characteristic example of his stylishness—a wonderful satin finish, spiralling complexity, and a soaring grace reminiscent of Giambologna's *Mercury*.

France owed its early acquisition of Mannerist sculptural style to Italian artists at Fontainebleau, to Primaticcio's stucco style, and to Cellini. Jean Goujon began from this point of inspiration, and his decorations for the *Fountain of the Innocents* (1547–49) possess a sophisticated refinement *all'antica* unequalled by any non-Italian artist of the period. Germain Pilon's elegant *Monument for the Heart of Henry II* was probably completed under Primaticcio's supervision. Pilon's statues for Primaticcio's Tomb of Henry II show him moving toward greater naturalism and expressiveness. In his later works Pilon achieved a freedom of plasticity and feeling for texture that anticipated Baroque developments.

With the advent of Bartolomé Ordóñez, Diego de Siloé, and the painter-sculptors Pedro Machuca and Alonso Berruguete, a native Spanish school of Mannerism was formed. Berruguete began to develop an elaborately pictorial style in sculptural complexes of great originality on his return to Spain (c. 1517) after studying in Italy. The fluid quality of his designs reaches its peak in the surging motions of the *Transfiguration Altar* (1543–48) for Toledo Cathedral. Berruguete's greatest successor at Valladolid was Pompeo Leoni, who collaborated with his father, Leone, on portraits of Charles V, composed in a disciplined and sternly Roman style.

BERNINI AND THE ITALIAN BAROQUE PERIOD

Gian Lorenzo Bernini, the greatest sculptor of the 17th and 18th centuries, established the sculptural principles for those two centuries in a series of youthful works of unrivalled virtuosity, as the *Apollo and Daphne*. Stone was now completely emancipated from stoniness by open form and by an astonishing illusion of flesh, hair, cloth, and other textures, pictorial effects that had earlier been attempted only in painting. These qualities made what his contemporaries called his "speaking portraits" seem unprecedentedly alive; portrait sculpture for two centuries was a variation of these innovations. In the statue of St. Longinus in St. Peter's in Rome, Bernini created the characteristic formula of Baroque sculpture by throwing the draperies into a violent turmoil, the complicated and broken involutions of which are not rationally explained by the figure's real bodily movement but seem paroxysmally informed by the miracle itself. The passion with which he imbued his sculptured figures, capturing the most transitory states of mind, reached its apogee in the representation of the ecstasy of St. Teresa in the Cornaro Chapel, Sta. Maria della Vittoria, Rome (1645–52) and in the figure of the expiring Ludovica Albertoni in the

Bernini's *The Ecstasy of St. Teresa*, in Santa Maria della Vittoria, in Rome. The framed pictorial scene, made up of sculpture, painting, and light, includes the worshipper in a religious drama.

Altieri Chapel, S. Francesco a Ripa, Rome (c. 1674). The former is generally considered the masterpiece of Baroque religious sculpture and shows how Bernini could organize the arts of architecture, painting, and sculpture in an overwhelming assault on the senses that dispels the resistance of the intellect. This ambitious plan was typical of the mature Bernini, whose spiritual and artistic aspirations exceeded the scope of his early secular salon statues. His later works were largely religious and unprecedentedly vast in scale, as in the dazzling *Cathedra Petri*, or Throne of St. Peter, which covers the whole end of St. Peter's in Rome with a teeming multitude of figures.

The tombs of Bernini are magnificent spectacles in which symbolic figures, clothed in sweeping draperies, with rhetorical gesture and expressive features, share in some emotional experience, theatrically depicted. An example is the tomb of Alexander VII in St. Peter's, Rome. The pontiff, set in a great apse, kneels on a high pedestal about which Charity, Truth, Justice, and Wisdom weep disconsolately while Death, a skeleton, raises the great draperies of polychrome and gold that veil a darkened doorway. Another work, the fountain of the Triton in the Piazza Barberini, Rome, from which all clarity of profile or of shadow, all definiteness of plane, are removed, is also characteristic of Bernini's style, widely imitated throughout Europe.

Bernini's art was the basis of all Baroque sculpture, but his example was not always followed, and the work of his more restrained contemporaries, such as Alessandro Algardi (relief of *Meeting of Attila and Pope Leo*, 1646–53) and the Fleming François Duquesnoy, attracted more approval from theorists of art. The latter's *St. Susanna* in Sta. Maria di Loreto in Rome, a figure after the antique but enlivened with Berninian textures, was originally made to look toward the observer and, with a gesture, to direct his attention to the altar. The distinction between art and life that the Mannerists had cultivated was banished by this active participation of the statue in the viewer's space and activities, another important innovation of Bernini.

LATE ITALIAN BAROQUE

A more or less classical late Baroque style, best exemplified by the heroic works of Camillo Rusconi in Rome, was dominant in central Italy through the middle of the 18th century. Rusconi's work had considerable influence outside Italy as well.

The latter half of the century saw the emergence of a much lighter and more theatrical manner in the works of Agostino Cornacchini and of Pietro Bracci, whose allegorical figure *Ocean* on the Fontana di

Trevi by Niccolò Salvi is almost a parody of Bernini's sculpture. Filippo della Valle worked in a classicizing style of almost French sensibility, but the majority of Italian sculpture of the mid-18th century became increasingly picturesque with a strong tendency toward technical virtuosity. Complex sculptured groups designed by Luigi Vanvitelli for the park of the palace at Caserta (c. 1770) are almost *tableaux vivants* ("living pictures") in a landscape setting, while the Cappella Sansevero de' Sangri in nearby Naples (decorated 1749–66) is one of the most important sculptured complexes of the time. Allegorical groups by Antonio Corradini and Francesco Queirolo vie with each other in virtuosity and include such conceits as fishnets cut from solid marble and the all-revealing shrouds developed by Giuseppe Sammartino.

Florentine sculpture of the 18th century is less spectacular, and Giovanni Battista Foggini took back from Rome the compromise style of Ferrarza, while Massimiliano Soldani-Benzi seems to have been instrumental in the brilliant revival there of small-scale bronze statuettes. Giovanni Marchiori worked in Venice with an attractive painterly style, in part based on the wood carvings of Andrea Brustolon; and Giovanni Maria Morlaiter ran the full gamut to a late 18th-century classicism close to the early works of the great Neoclassical sculptor Antonio Canova.

BAROQUE AND ROCOCO IN FRANCE

Duquesnoy was much admired in France, where the sculptors of Louis XIV (the "Sun King"), such as François Girardon, continued his tradition of setting correct and charming allusions to the antique in a pictorial and spatial context that is wholly Baroque. Girardon's tomb of the Cardinal de Richelieu, in the church of the Sorbonne, Paris, is illustrative of the Baroque monuments of France, calmer and more conservative than those of Italy. The dying cardinal, lying on his sarcophagus and originally gesturing in supplication toward the altar, is upheld by Religion and mourned by Science. The three figures, united by the lines of skillfully arranged draperies, are informed by a solemn and touching sentiment. The academic discipline imposed by the Sun King's ministers, especially Colbert, discouraged less tractable spirits, such as the passionate genius Pierre Puget. His unique expressions of anguish are couched in the physical terms of highly original works like the *Milo of Crotona*; here the composition of a figure rigid with pain is given an almost unbearable tension.

Antoine Coysevox, another of the sculptors of Louis XIV, had begun in the official "academic Baroque" style, but his later works, undertaken after the death of Colbert, are witnesses of the gradual acceptance of the Baroque in France, which now acquired the artistic leadership that Italy had long held over the rest of Europe. At the same time, the style was made lighter, gayer, and more ornamental, in accordance with 18th-century taste, as seen in the famous *Chevaux de Marly* by Guillaume Coustou, now marking the entrance to the Champs-Élysées in Paris. Coustou's bust of his brother Nicolas has a characteristic freshness and informality whereby 18th-century artists avoided the grandeur they found pompous in the Berninian tradition.

Coustou's style was narrative and dramatic, with some affinity to Rococo works. The rococo style originated in Paris in the early 18th century. It is characterized by lightness, elegance, and an exuberant use of curving, natural forms in ornamentation. The word "Rococo" is derived from the French word *rocaille*, which denoted the shell-covered rock work that was used to decorate artificial grottoes.

At the same time, the more classical current of French sculpture continued and gained importance as the 18th century advanced. The clarified form and continuous, unbroken contours of Étienne-Maurice Falconet's marble *Bather* (1757) adapt the Classic tradition to a pretty and intimate Rococo ideal that is the quintessence of 18th-century taste. This Classicism was purified by Jean-Antoine Houdon, who avoided the playful air of the Rococo in his *Diana* (c. 1777). His portrait sculptures are the ultimate in the 18th-century refinement of Bernini's tradition.

The little marble *Mercure* (1741) of Jean-Baptiste Pigalle is almost wholly Berninian, except in its intimacy and deliberate unpretentiousness. The narrative and indeed the allegory of Jean-Baptiste Pigalle's masterpiece, the tomb of the Maréchal de Saxe (1753), is as enthralling and memorable as any 17th-century sculpture, although the theme, significantly, no longer seems to be inspired by the Christian faith.

BAROQUE AND ROCOCO IN CENTRAL EUROPE

While the influence of Giambologna persisted in some quarters, Hans Krumper and Hans Reichle produced bronze figures less indebted to the Classical tradition but with stronger individuality. Jörg Zürn, whose finest wood carvings are to be seen at Überlingen, and Ludwig Münsterman, in Oldenburg, continued in the Mannerist style. Georg Petel, who came under the influence of Flemish painter Peter Paul Rubens, is almost the only sculptor to reveal the impact of the Baroque. Petel's importance lies mainly in his ivories, and Leonard Kern in Franconia developed a similar Rubensian style for his small statuettes.

LATIN AMERICA

With the coming of Europeans to Central and South America, indigenous symbolism and sculptural forms blended with Renaissance realism, Baroque elegance, and subsequent stylistic currents. Indian traits appeared in such European-introduced sculptural forms as the stone crosses that were erected in churchyards; statues, whether by European sculpture or aboriginal pupils, depicted Jesus, the Virgin Mary, saints, and occasionally an earthly benefactor of the church. Materials were of wood, plant fibre pulp coated with canvas and gesso, or plaster. The statues often had real costumes and hair, glass eyes and teeth, and extremely realistic flesh—bloody, bruised, and torn—with taut muscles and distended veins. Gold halos or crowns were added and costume textures were imitated by the gold-leaf-and-paint estofado technique. Many of these were undoubtedly inspired by paintings brought from Europe.

Few sculptors are known by name from the colonial period and fewer attributions are possible. At least a dozen individuals can be identified in Mexico in the 16th century, however, and twice that number in the 17th; the best known are José Cora of Puebla and his nephew Zacarias, and Gudiño of Querétaro. Many were both sculptors and architects, a necessity of the times.

The Baroque tradition tended to last until well into the 19th century in sculptures such as the robust figures of António Francisco Lisboa, the greatest sculptor that Brazil has produced.

Painting and sculpture recovered slowly from the ravages of the Thirty Years' War, and some of the earliest reflections of the high Baroque of Bernini are to be found in the sculpture of Matthias Rauchmiller at Trier (1675) and Legnica (Liegnitz) in Silesia (1677).

Among sculptors in Austria the forces of Classicism were stronger; and the weak north Italian late Baroque styles of Giovanni Giuliani and Lorenzo Mattielli were supplanted by the cool elegance and classical refinement of Georg Raphael Donner. His preference for the soft sheen of lead gave Austrian Baroque sculpture one of its most distinctive features.

During the first four decades of the 18th century, Bohemian Baroque art developed almost independently of Vienna. The brilliant rugged stone sculptures of Matyás Bernard Braun and Ferdinand Maximilián Brokoff, with their dynamism and expressive gestures, were truly Bohemian in spirit.

Bavarian Baroque art in the hands of the brothers Egid Quirin Asam and Cosmas Damian Asam was almost entirely confined to churches, and their brilliant development of the theatrical illusionism of Bernini is achieved in the high altar of the monastery church at Rohr, Germany, (1718–25), and in St. John Nepomuk in Munich (begun 1733). The sculptural style of Egid Quirin was formed on the south German tradition of wood carving, as well as on Bernini.

In Upper Saxony there was also a native tradition before the arrival of Permoser, represented by the heavy figures of Georg Heermann and Konrad Max Süssner, both of whom had been active in Prague in the 1680s. Balthasar Permoser was trained in Florence under Foggini, whence he was summoned to Dresden in 1689. His painterly conception of sculpture, derived from Bernini, is revealed in the complex *Apotheosis of Prince Eugene* (1721) and above all in the sculptural decoration of the Zwinger in Dresden initiated during the second decade. Paul Egell was a pupil of Permoser in Dresden at the time of the Zwinger decorations, and in 1721 he was appointed court sculptor at Mannheim. Egell's elongated and refined Baroque figures were an effective counter to the Classicism of Donner, and his personality was decisive in Franconia and the Palatinate during the first half of the century.

Berlin under the Great Elector of Brandenburg had become an increasingly important centre, both politically and artistically; and the full-bodied Baroque style of Andreas Schlüter, as revealed by his equestrian monument to the Great Elector (1696–1708), now at Charlottenburg, was fully in sympathy with the time.

No hard and fast division can be made between the Baroque and the Rococo in central and eastern Europe, either chronologically or stylistically. The first Rococo decorative ensembles in Germany, the Reiche Zimmer of the Residenz in Munich, were built by the Frenchman François de Cuvilliés in 1730–37, but in painting and sculpture the situation is more complicated. Ignaz Günther, the greatest south German sculptor of the 18th century, was trained under Johann Baptist Straub; the elongated forms of Egell's sculpture at Mannheim, however,

Günther's *Guardian Angel* (1763), a painted wood sculpture in the Bürgersaal, in Munich.

deeply impressed him, and his development was toward an almost Mannerist grace and refinement. Günther was capable of the most extraordinarily sensitive characterization of surfaces, even when painted white; and this he combined with an interpretation of character comparable to the late Gothic sculptors, thus giving his figures a realism and immediacy that is almost uncanny. Apart from their lightness and vivacity, however, it is the figures' relationship to the altars on which they are placed that reveals their Rococo quality. Gone are the great coordinated ensembles of the Asam brothers, and instead each figure has a totally separate existence of its own and a balance is only to be found when the church interior is taken as a whole.

Swabian sculpture of the period is characterized by the extremely successful partnerships between sculptors and stucco artists. For the abbeys of Zwiefalten and Ottobeuren, Joseph Christian provided the models from which Johann Michael Feichtmayr created the superb series of larger than life-size saints and angels that are the glory of these Rococo interiors. Feichtmayr was a member of the group of families from Wessobrunn in southern Bavaria that specialized in stucco work and produced a long series of masters, including Johann Georg Übelherr and Joseph Anton Feuchtmayer, whose masterpieces are the Rococo figures at the Birnau basilica on Lake Constance. The sculptor Christian Wenzinger worked at Freiburg im Breisgau in relative isolation, but his softly modelled figures have a delicacy that recalls the paintings of Boucher.

Until his death Johann Wolfgang van der Auvera was the most powerful personality in the field of sculpture in the area, but later Ferdinand Dietz at Bamberg pursued an increasingly individual Rococo style that often parodied the growing taste for Neoclassicism. Prussian Rococo sculpture was less distinguished, though the decorations of Johann August Nahl are among the most imaginative in Germany.

Austrian sculpture of the later 18th century, as represented by Balthasar Ferdinand Moll, inclined more toward a realistic Rococo style than to the Classicism of Donner; and, although the strange, neurotic genius Franz Xaver Messerschmidt began in this style, at the end of his career he produced a startling series of grimacing heads when he lived as a recluse in Bratislava.

CHAPTER FIVE

NEOCLASSICAL, ROMANTIC, AND MODERN SCULPTURE

The 18th-century arts movement known as Neoclassicism represents both a reaction against the last phase of the Baroque and, perhaps more importantly, a reflection of the burgeoning scientific interest in classical antiquity. Archaeological investigations of the classical Mediterranean world offered to the 18th-century cognoscenti compelling witness to the order and serenity of Classical art and provided a fitting backdrop to the Enlightenment and the Age of Reason.

Romanticism characterized many works of art from the late 18th to the mid-19th century. It is often seen as a rejection of the precepts of order, calm, harmony, balance, idealization, and rationality that typified Classicism in general and late 18th-century Neoclassicism in particular.

Modern art is the art of the 20th and 21st centuries and of the later part of the

19th century. It embraces a wide variety of movements, theories, and attitudes whose modernism resides particularly in a tendency to reject traditional, historical, or academic forms and conventions in an effort to create an art more in keeping with changed social, economic, and intellectual conditions.

NEOCLASSICISM

The accessibility of the sculpture of antiquity, in museums and private houses and also through engravings and plaster casts, had a far-reaching formative influence on 18th-century painting and sculpture. Successful excavations contributed to the rapid growth of collections of antique sculptures. The great majority of ancient sculptures collected were Roman, although many of them were copied from Greek originals and were believed to be Greek.

The ideals of Neoclassical sculpture—its emphasis on clarity of contour, on the plain ground, on not rivalling painting either in the imitation of aerial or linear perspective in relief or of flying hair and fluttering drapery in freestanding figures—were chiefly inspired by theory and by Roman neo-Attic works, or indeed by Roman pseudo-Archaic art. The latter class of art exerted an influence on John Flaxman, who was enormously admired for the severe style of his engravings and relief carvings.

"DECORUM" AND IDEALIZATION

Academic theorists, especially those of France and Italy during the 17th century, argued that the costume, details, and setting of a work be as accurate as possible when representing a period and place in the historical past. The 18th century and, in particular, the Neoclassicists inherited this theory of "decorum" and, enabled by all the newly available archaeological evidence, implemented it more fully than had any of their precursors.

A series of monuments to 18th- and early 19th-century generals and admirals of the Napoleonic Wars in St. Paul's Cathedral and Westminster Abbey demonstrate an important Neoclassical problem: whether a hero or famous person should be portrayed in Classical or contemporary costume. Many sculptors varied between showing the figures in uniform and showing them completely naked. The concept of the modern hero in antique dress belongs to the tradition of academic theory, exemplified by the English painter and aesthetician Sir Joshua Reynolds: "The desire for transmitting to posterity the shape of modern dress must be acknowledged to be purchased at a prodigious price, even the price of everything that is valuable in art." Even the living hero could be idealized completely naked, as in two colossal standing figures of Napoleon (1808–11) by the Italian sculptor Antonio Canova. One of the most famous of Neoclassical sculptures is Canova's *Paolina Borghese as Venus Victrix* (1805–07). She is shown naked, lightly draped, and reclining sensuously on a couch, both a charming contemporary portrait and an idealized antique Venus.

RELATION TO THE BAROQUE AND THE ROCOCO

Classical academic theories circulating in the Renaissance, and especially in the 17th century, favoured the antique and those artists who followed in this tradition. The exuberance and "fury" of the Baroque must be avoided, it was argued, because they led to "barbarous" and "wicked" works. Continuing in this tradition, Johann Joachim Winckelmann, the great German historian of ancient art, argued that the Italian Baroque sculptor and architect Bernini had been "misled" by following nature.

Such hostility to Baroque works, however, did not immediately eradicate their influence on 18th-century artists, as can be seen in an early work by Canova, *Daedalus and Icarus*

(1779), executed before he had been to Rome. In Canova's tomb of Pope Clement XIV (1784–87), the Pope, seated on a throne above a sarcophagus, is treated in a dramatically realistic style with hand raised in a forceful gesture reminiscent of papal tombs of the 17th century.

Although the Neoclassical artists and writers expressed contempt for what they regarded as the frivolous aspect of the Rococo, there is a strong influence of French Rococo on the early style of some of the Neoclassical sculptors. Étienne-Maurice Falconet, Flaxman, and Canova all started to carve and model with Rococo tendencies, which were then gradually transformed into more Classical elements.

LEADING FIGURES

Gestures and emotions in Neoclassical works are usually restrained. In bacchanalian scenes the gaiety is held in check, never bursting into exuberance. Prominent early British Neoclassicist sculptors included John Wilton, Joseph Nollekens, John Bacon the Elder, John Deare, and Christopher Hewetson, the last two working mostly in Rome. The leading artist of the younger generation was John Flaxman, professor of sculpture at the Royal Academy in London. The last generation of Neoclassicists included the sculptors Sir Richard Westmacott, John Bacon the Younger, Sir Francis Chantrey, Edward Hodges Baily, John Gibson, and William Behnes.

While Neoclassicism in France was dominated by painting and architecture, the movement did find a number of notable exponents in sculpture. These included Claude Michel, called Clodion, creator of many small Classical figures, especially nymphs; Augustin Pajou; and Pierre Julien. Pigalle's pupil Jean-Antoine Houdon was the most famous 18th-century French sculptor, producing many Classical figures and contemporary portraits in the manner of antique busts. Other contemporary sculptors included Louis-Simon Boizot and Étienne-Maurice Falconet, who was director of sculpture at the Sèvres factory. The slightly younger generation included the sculptors Joseph Chinard, Joseph-Charles Marin, Antoine-Denis Chaudet, and Baron François-Joseph Bosio. The early sculpture of Ingres's well-known contemporary François Rude was Neoclassical.

Important among central European sculptors early in the period was Johann Heinrich von Dannecker. Subsequent Neoclassicists included Johann Gottfried Schadow, who was also a painter but is better known as a sculptor; his pupil, the sculptor Christian Friedrich Tieck; the painter and sculptor Martin von Wagner; and the sculptor Christian Daniel Rauch.

Canova's *Paolina Borghese as Venus Victrix*, now located in the Galleria Borghese, in Rome, shows its subject reclining on a couch in a fusion of classical goddess and contemporary portrait.

The most important Italian Neoclassicist was Antonio Canova, the leading sculptor, indeed by far the most famous artist of any sort, in Europe by the end of the 18th century. Canova's position in the following 20 years may be compared only with that enjoyed by Bernini in the 17th century. The differences between their careers, however, are of great importance. Only at the commencement of his career did Bernini carve gallery sculpture for princely collectors, but the majority of Canova's works belong to this category. Both artists remained resident for most of their life in Rome, but whereas Bernini was controlled by the popes and only rarely permitted to work for foreign potentates, Canova's principal patrons were foreigners, and he supplied sculpture to all the courts of Europe. A fine sculptor of varying styles, including austere, sentimental, and horrific, Canova produced an extensive body of work that includes Classical groups and friezes, tombs, and portraits, many in antique dress. Other Neoclassical sculptors in Rome included Canova's pupil and collaborator, Antonio d'Este, and Giuseppe Angelini, best known for the tomb of the etcher and architect Giambattista Piranesi in the church of Sta. Maria del Priorato, Rome.

In Milan, Camillo Pacetti directed the sculptural decoration of the Arco della Pace. The work of Gaetano Monti, born in Ravenna, can be seen in many northern Italian churches. The Tuscan sculptor Lorenzo Bartolini executed some important Napoleonic commissions. The *Charity* is one of the more famous examples of his later Neoclassicism. It should be noted, however, that he did not see himself as a Neoclassical artist and that he challenged the idealism that was favoured by Canova and his followers.

The Swede Johan Tobias Sergel, court sculptor to the Swedish king Gustav III, and the Dane Bertel Thorvaldsen, who lived most of his life in Rome, were among the best-known Neoclassical sculptors in Europe. Thorvaldsen was the chief rival to Canova and eventually replaced him in critical favour. His work was more severe, sometimes even archaizing in character, and his religious sculpture, most notably his great figure of Christ in the Church of Our Lady in Copenhagen, exhibits a deliberately chilling, sublime style that still awaits sympathetic reassessment. Among his more notable pupils was the Swedish sculptor Johan Byström.

Both leading Russian Neoclassicists were sculptors. Ivan Petrovich Martos studied under Mengs, Thorvaldsen, and Pompeo Batoni in Rome and became a director of the St. Petersburg Academy. His most praised works are tombs. Mikhail Kozlovskij contributed to the decoration of the throne room at Pavlovsk.

Most of the leading Neoclassicists among American artists were sculptors. William Rush produced standing Classical figures including those formerly decorating a waterworks in Philadelphia. In the middle years of the 19th century there came into prominence four sculptors: Horatio Greenough, who executed several government commissions in Washington, D.C.; Hiram Powers, known particularly for his portrait busts; Thomas Crawford, who did monumental sculpture; and William Wetmore Story, who lived and worked in Rome, where he was associated with several other prominent 19th-century Americans.

19TH-CENTURY SCULPTURE

In the 19th century sculptors throughout the Western world were affected in an unprece-dented way by the great public annual exhibitions organized by the Academies. Great patrons at court or among the nobility could still play a very important part in making an artist's reputation, but publicity from these exhibitions was crucial.

The old clichés about "academic" sculpture in the 19th century are hopelessly inadequate. The Academies in their educational program often encouraged a heroic but restrained Neoclassicism—their exhibitions, on the other hand, encouraged an appeal to novelty, to sentiment, and to sensationalism, involving subjects from modern life and modern literature.

The exhibition piece was often a plaster cast of the original clay model. Several versions in marble or bronze were then made if there was the demand. These would be acquired for the sculpture galleries, conservatories, or gardens of great collectors, as well as for museums, which, for the first time, included collections of modern art. In reduced form they might also make an appearance amid the crowded furnishings of fashionable drawing rooms. Upon the chimneypiece perhaps some miniature scene of jungle violence modelled by Antoine-Louis Barye and cast in bronze might be displayed while behind the ferns a marble nude would shrink in vain from male scrutiny.

The proliferation of domestic sculpture was made possible by a series of technical innovations chiefly associated with Paris.

Improved reducing machines greatly facilitated the half-size replication of exhibition pieces and the reproduction of such works on a still smaller scale as bronze statuettes. New methods of sand-casting meant that these bronzes were also available in larger editions and at a lower cost. The reproduction of terra-cotta sculpture also thrived in Paris as it had done in the late 18th century; busts of men of letters and women of fashion, together with groups of seductive nymphs, were always the most popular subjects. The miniature sculptures (often also reproductions of larger works) in biscuit porcelain, which had also been produced in 18th-century Paris, also continued to be popular in England and France.

Mechanical methods—more and more sophisticated machinery for turning and pointing, as well as reducing machinery and novel techniques of casting—were often employed with great success. In Paris, the fertile genius of Albert Carrier-Belleuse particularly excelled in devising such objects as gasoliers (gaslight chandeliers) supported by pretty girls in a luxurious style that combined elements from the art of the 16th, 17th, and 18th centuries. In England, sculptor Alfred Stevens, inspired by the versatility of the Italian Renaissance, also designed cutlery and fire grates. At the end of the century, Alfred Gilbert, creator of the most remarkable metropolitan fountain since the Renaissance (the *Eros* in Piccadilly Circus), also devoted himself wholeheartedly to the art of the goldsmith.

One aspect of 19th-century sculpture was the large-scale relief panels and pedimental ornaments and niche stances on churches and public buildings. Another type of public sculpture—the portrait, typically in bronze, erected in a town square or other public space—flourished in the 19th century as it had not done since the first centuries CE. The first prominent sculptures of this sort commemorating nonroyal figures since antiquity seem to have appeared in Britain. The statues of Admiral Lord Nelson by Sir Richard Westmacott erected in Liverpool and Birmingham soon after the subject's death were followed by statues of political heroes such as Charles James Fox (1816) and William Pitt (1819). By the end of the century, even relatively minor generals, philanthropists, or entrepreneurs were commemorated in this manner—almost invariably at the expense of public subscribers. The rest of Europe eventually followed this English example.

The young countries of the New World—the United States and later the republics of Latin America—commemorated with statues heroes whom they perceived as national saviours and founders. It may be that statues of Nelson excited as much patriotic sentiment as those of Washington or Bolívar, but Nelson could not embody the nation as the others did, nor certainly could any statue of a European monarch. Among the most remarkable public sculpture of the 19th century must certainly be counted Carlo Marochetti's *Duke Emmanuel Philibert* (1833, Turin) and Christian Daniel Rauch's *Frederick the Great* (1836–51, Berlin) and the several statues of Joan of Arc in France. These were works of not simply historical but also topical and political significance, as indeed was the colossal *Christ of the Andes* by Mateo Alonso erected in 1902 on the border of Chile and Argentina. Abstractions were also endowed with a more urgent ideological content than in former centuries. One example is the great *Triumph of the Republic* by Jules Dalou, unveiled in 1899 at Paris's Place de la Nation.

In the 19th century, funeral sculpture was as completely revolutionized as public sculpture. Whereas previously it had only been in England that a large section of the wealthier classes had enjoyed the privilege of erecting substantial sculptured memorials, the opening up of large landscaped municipal cemeteries made this possible elsewhere. These cemeteries, of which the finest examples are in Paris and in Italy, were free from ecclesiastical censorship, and new themes quickly developed that were appropriate for an age of doubt and of desperate faith. The sentimentality

AUGUSTUS SAINT-GAUDENS

Generally acknowledged to be the foremost American sculptor of the late 19th century, Augustus Saint-Gaudens was noted for his evocative memorial statues and for the subtle modeling of his low reliefs. Born in Ireland to a French father and an Irish mother, Saint-Gaudens's family moved to New York City when he was an infant. In 1867 he was admitted to the École des Beaux-Arts and became one of the first Americans to study sculpture in Paris. After spending time in Rome, he settled in New York, where he befriended and collaborated with a circle of men who formed the nucleus of an American artistic renaissance. The most important work of Saint-Gaudens's early career was the monument to Admiral David Farragut (1880, Madison Square Park, New York), the base of which was designed by Sanford White.

From 1880 to 1897 Saint-Gaudens executed most of the well-known works that gained him his great reputation and many honours. In 1887 he began the *Amor Caritas*, which, with variations, preoccupied him from about 1880 to 1898, and also a statue of a standing Abraham Lincoln (Lincoln

Park, Chicago). The memorial to Mrs. Henry Adams (1891) in Rock Creek Cemetery, Washington, D.C., is considered by many to be Saint-Gaudens's greatest work. In 1897 Saint-Gaudens completed a monument in Boston depicting Robert G. Shaw, colonel of an African American regiment in the Civil War. The statue is remarkable for its expression of movement.

and sensationalism of the annual exhibition were found here also, and so too was much exhibitionist virtuosity devoted to depicting the veiled faces and figures of ascending souls and their androgynous angelic escorts.

This virtuosity is largely associated with Italian sculpture; and in a sense the Italians continued to dominate sculpture throughout the Western world after the death of Canova, by supplying the skilled carvers who were everywhere employed to translate into marble ideas worked out in clay. The sculptors of the 19th century tended to play a smaller part than any of their predecessors in the actual carving, and the most vital sculpture of the period is preeminently plastic (moldable): when one thinks of the broken surfaces of the portrait busts by Jean-Baptiste Carpeaux, for example, or of the precarious balances, open forms, and eloquent contours of Gilbert's statuettes, one thinks of wax and clay.

MODERN SCULPTURE

The origins of modern art are usually traced to the mid-19th-century rejection of Academic tradition in subject matter and style by certain artists and critics. Painters of the Impressionist school that emerged in France in the late 1860s sought to free painting from the tyranny of the subject and to explore the intrinsic qualities of colour, brushwork, and form. This expansive notion of visual rendering had revolutionary effects on sculpture as well. The French sculptor Auguste Rodin found in it a new basis for life modelling and thus restored to the art a stylistic integrity that it had hardly possessed for more than two centuries.

RODIN AND HIS CONTEMPORARIES

Rodin's highly naturalistic early work, *The Age of Bronze* (1877), is effective because the banal studio pose of a man leaning on a staff produced an unconventional and expressive gesture when the staff was removed. From French painter and draughtsman Honoré Daumier, Rodin had learned the bold modelling of surfaces that are emotive rather than literal; the statue is only a rough approximation that avoids the definitive finish of earlier sculpture and remains in a state of becoming. Eventually,

Rodin even worked with mere fragments such as broken torsos, and he enlarged the range of figure composition. The mass, until then the principal vehicle of sculptural composition, was explosively opened by these methods; in contrast to earlier sculpture, which depended on the interplay of solid and void, Rodin's works are fused with the surrounding space. These methods evolved in his many

Rodin's *The Three Shades*, outside the Musée Rodin, in Paris. This is a later casting of a work initially meant to stand atop of *The Gates of Hell* and originally modelled between 1880 and 1904.

works, such as *Adam* (1880), *Eve* (1881), and others, originally conceived as a part of the masterpiece of modern sculpture, *The Gates of Hell*, undertaken by Rodin in 1880 and never really completed. It was inevitable that the translucent nature of the marble surface should engage the attention of Rodin, and even though he always prepared the models in clay and left the execution in stone to assistants, such marbles as *The Kiss* (1885), when properly exhibited with light partly from the rear, appear to glow with the incandescence of their passionate intensity.

Among Rodin's contemporaries, Edgar Degas, whose sculpture, begun in the 1880s, was an intimate study of movement and light, in several respects predicts 20th-century developments. Rodin's Italian counterpart, Medardo Rosso, lived in Paris during the 1880s. Rosso used wax in such a way that light was suffused through sensitively modelled portraits, and labile forms were created to express the flux that he felt was a condition of modern life. In Italy Rosso influenced Arturo Martini and through him Giacomo Manzù, Marino Marini, and Alberto Viani.

Two of the many young sculptors attracted to Paris by Rodin's fame were Wilhelm Lehmbruck and Constantin Brancusi. Lehmbruck's early work has the soft modelling by touches of clay characteristic of the time, as in his *Mother and Child* (1907) and *Bust of a Woman* (1910).

Brancusi's *Sleeping Muse* (1908) and the small *Bust of a Boy with Head Inclined* (1907) reflect Rodin's later interests in the expressiveness of modelling as opposed to strenuous gesture. Pablo Picasso and Henri Matisse were also early disciples of Rodin, as was Sir Jacob Epstein, particularly in his naturalistic and psychologically incisive portraits.

AVANT-GARDE SCULPTURE (1909–20)

In the second decade of the 20th century, the tradition of body rendering extending from the Renaissance to Rodin was shattered, and Brancusi, the Cubists, and the Constructivists emerged as the most influential forces. Cubism, with its compositions of imagined rather than observed forms and relationships, had a similarly marked influence.

Among the first examples of the revolutionary sculpture is Picasso's *Woman's Head* (1909). The sculptor no longer relied upon traditional methods of sculpture or upon his sensory experience of the body; what was given to his outward senses of sight and touch was dominated by strong conceptualizing. The changed and forceful appearance of the head derives from the use of angular planar volumes joined in a new syntax independent of anatomy. In contrast to traditional portraiture, the eyes and mouth are less expressive than the forehead, cheeks, nose, and hair. Matisse's head of *Jeanette* (1910–11) also partakes of a personal reproportioning that gives a new vitality to the less mobile areas of the face. Likewise influenced by the Cubists' manipulation of their subject matter, Alexander Archipenko in his *Woman Combing Her Hair* (1915) rendered the body by means of concavities rather than convexities and replaced the solid head by its silhouette within which there is only space.

Brancusi also abandoned Rodin's rhetoric and reduced the body to its mystical inner core. His *The Kiss* (1908), with its two blocklike figures joined in symbolic embrace, has a concentration of expression comparable to that of primitive art. In this and subsequent works Brancusi favoured hard materials and surfaces as well as self-enclosed volumes that often impart an introverted character to his subjects. His bronze *Bird in Space* became a cause célèbre in the 1920s when U.S. customs refused to admit it duty free as a work of art.

Raymond Duchamp-Villon began as a follower of Rodin, but his portrait head *Baudelaire* (1911) contrasts with that by his predecessor in its more radical departure from the flesh; the somewhat squared-off head is molded by clear, hard volumes. His famous *Horse* (1914), a coiled, vaguely mechanical form bearing little resemblance to the animal itself, suggests metaphorically the horsepower

Brancusi produced several versions of his *The Kiss*, including this plaster one that dates from 1908–09 and is in a private collection. The earliest version of *The Kiss* was carved from stone.

of locomotive drive shafts and, by extension, the mechanization of modern life. Duchamp-Villon may have been influenced by Umberto Boccioni, one of the major figures in the Italian Futurist movement and a sculptor who epitomized the Futurist love of force and energy deriving from the machine. Boccioni argued that the sculptor should model objects as they interact with their environment, thus revealing the dynamic essence of reality.

In 1913, after several years of conservative training, Jacques Lipchitz made a number of small bronzes experimenting with the compass curve and angular planes. They reveal an understanding of the Cubist reconstitution of the bodies in an impersonal quasi-geometric armature over which the artist exercised complete autonomy. Continuing to work in this fashion, he produced *Man with a Guitar* and *Standing Figure* (both 1915), in which voids are introduced, while in the early 1920s he developed freer forms more consistently based on curves.

Lehmbruck's mature style emerged in the *Kneeling Woman* (1911) and *Standing Youth* (1913), in which his gothicized, elongated bodies with their angular posturings and appearance of growing from the earth give expression to his notions of modern heroism. In contrast to this spiritualized view is his *The Fallen* (1915–16), intended as a compassionate memorial for friends lost in the war.

CONSTRUCTIVISM AND DADA

Between 1912 and 1914 there emerged an antisculptural movement, called Constructivism, that attacked the false seriousness and hollow moral ideals of academic art. The movement began with the relief fabrications of Vladimir Tatlin in 1913. The Constructivists and their sympathizers preferred industrially manufactured materials, such as plastics, glass, iron, and steel, to marble and bronze. Their sculptures were not formed by carving, modelling, and casting but by twisting, cutting, welding, or literally constructing: thus the name Constructivism.

Unlike traditional figural representation, the Constructivists' sculpture denied mass as a plastic element and volume as an expression of space; for these principles they substituted geometry and mechanics. In the machine, where the Futurists saw violence, the Constructivists saw beauty. Like their sculptures, it was something invented; it could be elegant, light, or complex, and it demanded the ultimate in precision and calculation.

Seeking to express pure reality, with the veneer of accidental appearance stripped away, the Constructivists fabricated objects totally devoid of sentiment or literary association; Naum Gabo's work frequently resembled mathematical models, and several Constructivist sculptures, such as those by

Kazimir Malevich and Georges Vantongerloo, have the appearance of architectural models. The Constructivists created, in effect, sculptural metaphors for the new world of science, industry, and production.

While Constructivism was one offshoot of the Cubist collage, a second was the fantastic object or Dadaist assemblage. The Dadaist movement, while sharing Constructivism's iconoclastic vigour, opposed its insistence upon rationality. Dadaist assemblages were, as the name suggests, "assembled" from materials lying about in the studio, such as wood, cardboard, nails, wire, and paper; examples are Kurt Schwitters's *Rubbish Construction* (1921) and Marcel Duchamp's *Disturbed Balance* (1918). This art generally exalted the accidental, the spontaneous, and the impulsive, giving free play to associations. Its paroxysmal and negativist tenor led its subscribers into other directions, but Dadaism formed the basis of the imaginative sculpture that emerged in the later 1920s.

In the 1920s modern art underwent a reaction comparable to the changes experienced by society as a whole. In the postwar search for security, permanence, and order, the earlier insurgent art seemed to many to be antithetical to these ends, and certain avant-garde artists radically changed their art and thought. Lipchitz's portraits *Gertrude*

Stein (1920) and *Berthe Lipchitz* (1922) return volume and features to the head but not an intimacy of contact with the viewer. Tatlin and Alexander Rodchenko broke with the Constructivists around 1920. British sculptor Jacob Epstein developed some of his finest naturalistic portraiture in this decade. Rudolph Belling abandoned the mechanization that had characterized his *Head* (1925) in favour of musculature and individual identity in his statue *Max Schmeling* of 1929. Matisse's reclining nudes and the "Back" series of 1929 show less violently worked surfaces and more massive and obvious structuring.

SCULPTURE OF FANTASY (1920–45)

Between World Wars I and II, an antirational artistic movement known as Surrealism grew out of Dadaism. One trend of Surrealist sculpture of the late 1920s and the 1930s consisted of compositions made up of found objects, such as Meret Oppenheim's *Object, Fur Covered Cup* (1936). As with Dadaist fabrications, the unfamiliar conjunction of familiar objects in these assemblies was dictated by impulse and irrationality and could be summarized by Isidore Ducasse's often-quoted statement, "Beautiful . . . as the chance meeting on a dissecting table of a sewing machine with an umbrella."

More significant was the sculpture of a second group that included Alberto Giacometti, Jean Arp, Lipchitz, Henry Moore, Barbara Hepworth, Picasso, Julio González, and Alexander Calder. Although these sculptors were sometimes in sympathy with Surrealist objectives, their aesthetic and intellectual concerns prohibited a more consistent attachment. Their art, derived from visions, hallucinations, reverie, and memory, might best be called the sculpture of fantasy. Giacometti's *Palace at 4 A.M.* interprets the artist's vision not in terms of the external public world but in an enigmatic, private language. Moore's series of *Forms* suggest shapes in the process of forming under the influence of each other and the medium of space. The appeal of primitive and ancient ritual art to Moore, the element of surprise in children's toys for Calder, and the wellsprings of irrationality from which Arp and Giacometti drank were for these men the means by which wonder and the marvelous could be restored to sculpture. While their works are often violent transmutations of life, their objectives were peaceful; " . . . to inject into the vain and bestial world and its retinue, the machines, something peaceful and vegetative."

OTHER SCULPTURE
(1920–45)

The sculpture of Moore, Gaston Lachaise, and Henri Laurens during the 1920s and '30s included mature, ripe human bodies, erogenic images reminiscent of Hindu sculpture, appearing inflated with breath rather than supported by skeletal armatures. Lachaise's *Montagne* (1934–35) and Moore's reclining nudes of the '30s and '40s are identifications with earth, growth, vital rhythm, and silent power. Prior to Moore and the work of Archipenko, Boccioni, and Lipchitz, space had been a negative element in figure sculpture; in Moore's string sculptures and Lipchitz's transparencies of the 1920s, it became a prime element of design.

Lipchitz's *Song Of The Vowels* (designed 1931-2, executed 1969), on the Princeton University campus.

Lipchitz's figure style of the late 1920s and '30s is inseparable from his emerging optimistic humanism. His concern with subject matter began with the ecstatic *Joy of Life* (1927). Thereafter his seminal themes were of love and security and assertive passionate acts that throw off the inertia of his Cubist figures. In the *Return of the Prodigal Son* (1931), for example, strong, facetted curvilinear volumes weave a pattern of emotional and aesthetic accord between parent and child.

American sculptor John B. Flannagan rendered animal forms as well as the human figure in a simple, almost naive style. His interest in what he called the "profound subterranean urges of the human spirit in the whole dynamic life process, birth, growth, decay and death" resulted in *Head of a Child* (1935), *New One* (1935), *Not Yet* (1940), and *The Triumph of the Egg* (1941).

Somewhat more mystical are Brancusi's *Beginning of the World* (1924), *Fish* (1928–30), and *The Seal* (1936). As with Flannagan, the recurrent egg form in Brancusi's art symbolizes the mystery of life. Nature in motion is the subject of Calder's mobiles, such as *Lobster Trap and Fish Tail* (1939) and others suggesting the movement of leaves, trees, and snow.

DEVELOPMENTS AFTER WORLD WAR II

As the artist Ibram Lassaw said, "The modern artist is the counterpart in our time of the alchemist-philosopher who once toiled over furnaces, alembics and crucibles, ostensibly to make gold, but who consciously entered the most profound levels of being, philosophizing over the melting and mixing of various ingredients" (Ibram Lassaw, quoted by Lawrence Campbell in *Art News*, p. 66, The Art Foundation Press, New York, March 1954). While work in the older mediums persisted, it was the welding, soldering, and cutting of metal that emerged after 1945 as an increasingly popular medium for sculpture.

Sculptors such as Peter Agostini, George Spaventa, Peter Grippe, David Slivka, and Lipchitz, who were interested in bringing spontaneity, accident, and automatism into play, returned to the more labile media of wax and clay, with occasional cire-perdue casting, which permit a very direct projection of the artist's feelings. By the nature of the processes such work is usually on a small scale.

A number of artists brought new technique and content to the Dadaist form of the assemblage. Among the most important was the American Joseph Cornell, who combined printed matter and three-dimensional objects in his intimately sealed, often enigmatic glass-fronted boxes.

WHY METAL?

The appeal of metal is manifold. It is plentifully available from commercial supply houses; it is flexible and permanent; it allows the artist to work quickly; and it is relatively cheap compared to casting. Industrial metals also relate modern sculpture physically, aesthetically, and emotionally to its context in modern civilization.

The basic tool of the metal sculptor is the oxyacetylene torch, which achieves a maximum temperature of 6,500° F (3,600° C; the melting point of bronze is 2,000° F). In the hands of a skilled artist the torch can cut or weld, harden or soften, colour and lighten or darken metal. Files, hammers, chisels, and jigs are also used in shaping the metal, worked either hot or cold. The sculptor may first construct a metal armature that he then proceeds to conceal or expose. He builds up his form with various metals and alloys, fusing or brazing them, and may expose parts or the whole to the chemical action of acids. This type of work requires constant control, and many sculptors work out and guard their own recipes.

Another modern phenomenon, seen particularly in Italy, France, and the United States, was the revival of relief sculpture and the execution of such works on a large scale, intended to stand alone rather than in conjunction with a building. Louise Nevelson, for example, typically employed boxes as container compartments in which she carefully placed an assortment of objects and then painted them a uniform colour. In Europe the outstanding metal reliefs were those by Alberto Burri, Gio and Arnaldo Pomodoro, César, Zoltán Kemény, and Manuel Rivera.

Development of metal sculpture, particularly in the United States, led to fresh interpretations of the natural world. In the art of Richard Lippold and Lassaw, the search for essential structures took the form of qualitative analogies. Lippold's *Full Moon* (1949–50) and *Sun* (1953–56) show an intuition of a basic regularity, precise order, and completeness that underlies the universe. Lassaw's comparable interest in astronomical phenomena inspired his *Planets* (1952) and *The Clouds of Magellan* (1953).

In contrast to the macrocosmic concern of these two artists were the interests of sculptors such as Raymond Jacobson, whose *Structure* (1955) derived from his study of honeycombs. Using three basic sizes, Jacobson constructed his sculpture of hollowed cubes emulating the modular, generally regular but slightly unpredictable formal quality of the honeycomb.

Isamu Noguchi's *Night Land* (1947) is one of the first pure landscapes in sculpture. David Smith's *Hudson River Landscape* (1951), Theodore J. Roszak's *Recollections of the Southwest* (1948), Louise Bourgeois's *Night Garden* (1953), and Leo Amino's *Jungle* (1950) are later examples.

THE HUMAN FIGURE SINCE WORLD WAR II

Once figural sculpture moved away from straightforward imitation, the human form was subjected to an enormous variety of interpretations. The thin, vertical, Etruscan idol-like figures developed by Giacometti showed his repugnance toward rounded, smooth body surfaces or strong references to the flesh. His men and women do not exist in felicitous concert with others; each form is a secret sanctum, a maximum of being wrested from a minimum of material. Reg Butler's work (e.g., *Woman Resting* [1951]) and that of David Hare (*Figure in a Window* [1955]) treat the body in terms of skeletal outlines. Butler's figures partake of nonhuman qualities and embody fantasies of an unsentimental and

Moore's *Two-Piece Reclining Figure No. 9* (1968), at the National Library of Australia, in Canberra. In this late piece, Moore continued to work out ideas that had long occupied his imagination.

aggressive character; the difficulties and tensions of existence are measured out in taut wire armatures and constricting malleable bronze surfaces. Kenneth Armitage and Lynn Chadwick, two other British sculptors, make the clothing a direct extension of the figure, part of a total gesture. In his *Family Going for a Walk* (1953), for example, Armitage creates a fanciful screenlike figure recalling wind-whipped clothing on a wash line. Both Chadwick and Armitage transfer the burden of expression from human limbs and faces to the broad planes of the bulk of the sculpture. Chadwick's sculptures are often illusive hybrids suggesting alternately impotent De

Chirico-like figures or animated geological forms.

Luciano Minguzzi admired the amply proportioned feminine form. Minguzzi's women (e.g., *Woman Jumping Rope* [1954]) exert themselves with a kind of playful abandon. Marini's women (e.g., *Dancer* [1949]) enjoy a stately passivity, their quiescent postures permitting a contrapuntal focus on the graceful transition from the slender extremities to the large, compact, voluminous torso, with small, rich surface textures.

The segmented torso, popular with Arp, Laurens, and Picasso earlier, continued to be reinterpreted by Alberto Viani, Bernard Heiliger, Karl Hartung, and Raoul Hague. The emphasis of these sculptors was upon more subtle, sensuous joinings that created self-enclosing surfaces. Viani's work, for example, does not glorify body culture or suggest macrocosmic affinities as does an ideally proportioned Phidian figure; his torsos are seen in a private way, as in his *Nude* (1951), with its large body and golf ball-sized breasts.

Among the most impressive figure sculptures made in the United States in the late 1950s were those by Seymour Lipton. Their large-scale, taut design and provocative interweaving of closed and open shapes restore qualities of mystery and the heroic to the human form.

ARCHAIZING, IDOL MAKING, AND RELIGIOUS SCULPTURE

After World War II several sculptors became interested in the art of early Mediterranean civilizations. The result was a conscious archaizing of the human form with the intent of recapturing qualities of Cycladic idols, early Greek and Egyptian statuary, and some aspects of late Roman art.

Moore's admiration for archaic Greek sculpture produced *Draped Reclining Figure* (1952), which shows his return to the solid form and the suggestion of power and force by using drapery as a tense foil for the volumes that press against it. His *King and Queen* (1952–53) resulted from further excursions into the archaic Greek myth world.

The interest in recreating idols or totems was continued by Arp in his *Idol* (1950) and by Noguchi in his Stone Age-type sculptures for the Connecticut General Life Insurance Company (now CIGNA Corporation, 1956). By creating presences that

Isamu Noguchi's *The Family* (1956), on the grounds of the CIGNA Corporation, Bloomfield, Connecticut.

elude rational definition, these artists restored to art its ancient aura of myth, mystery, and magic in an age that consistently disclaims their existence.

The argument that modern sculpture is inappropriate for religious requirements is disproved by the works of Lipchitz, Lassaw, and Herbert Ferber. In keeping with the Jewish preference for nonfigural art, Ferber's *. . . and the bush was not consumed* (1951), commissioned by a synagogue in Millburn, New Jersey, comprises clusters of branches and boldly shaped weaving flames, invisibly suspended in a powerful and intimate vision that absorbs its viewers with its hypnotic rhythm. Lassaw's *Pillar of Fire*, for the exterior of a synagogue in Springfield, Massachusetts, has a mesmerizing pattern recalling the illusory images sometimes seen in flames. Lipchitz's sculpture of the *Virgin of Assy* (1948–54) was commissioned for the Catholic church at Assy, France.

PUBLIC AND PRIVATE MEMORIALS

After World War II there was a flood of public memorial sculpture, and in Europe especially many of the commissions were carried out by modern sculptors. A striking war memorial in Italy is Mirko Basaldella's gate for the monument to the Roman hostages killed in the Ardeatine Caves (1951). For its full effect the gate must be seen in connection with the rugged masonry wall to which it is attached. The gate was cast in metal and fashioned in a tangled, thicket-like pattern that suggests the painfully difficult passage from life to death for those who died in the caves.

Another imposing memorial is Ossip Zadkine's *The Destroyed City* (c. 1947–51), a monument to the bombing of Rotterdam, in which a figure recoils from the violence that descended from the sky. In Moore's *Warrior with a Shield* (1953-54), a soldier defiantly raises his shield and mutilated body toward the ill-starred heavens during the *Battle of Britain* (1940). Epstein's public monument in Philadelphia, *Social Consciousness* (1952–53), treats the helplessness of those confronted with pressures over which they have no control.

MINIMALISM

Minimalism was a chiefly American movement in the visual arts and music that originated in New York City in the late 1960s and was characterized by extreme simplicity of form and a literal, objective approach.

Minimal art, also called ABC art, is the culmination of reductionist tendencies in modern art that first surfaced in the 1913 composition by the Russian painter Kasimir

Malevich of a black square on a white ground. Leading minimalist sculptors include Donald Judd, Carl Andre, Dan Flavin, Tony

Untitled (1989), by Donald Judd, at the Museum of Modern Art, in New York. After 1980 Judd's sculptures grew larger and more complex.

Smith, Richard Serra, Anthony Caro, Sol LeWitt, John McCracken, Craig Kaufman, Robert Duran, and Robert Morris.

Minimal sculpture is composed of extremely simple, monumental geometric forms made of fibreglass, plastic, sheet metal, or aluminum, either left raw or solidly painted with bright industrial colours. Minimalist sculptors attempted to make their works totally objective, unexpressive, and nonreferential.

POSTMODERNISM

Postmodernism—a multifaceted movement that took hold in the 1980s and extended into the 21st century—places its emphasis on radical exaggeration and self-awareness. Postmodern artists rejected the idea of the artist as genius and the notion of the supremacy in authenticity. In the work of the artist Jeff Koons, for instance, this postmodern rejection of the handmade or authentic is given a comic tone, at once eccentric and humorous. Koons was an early pioneer of appropriation—the use of pre-existing content—reproducing banal commercial images and objects with only slight modifications in scale or material. In the first decade of the 21st century, he was best known for his fabricated objects from commercial sources—primarily inflatable pool toys and balloon animals—in highly polished and coloured stainless steel. Koons established a large studio/factory in New York City's Chelsea neighbourhood, where dozens of employees produce the work that he conceives.

Another key postmodernist is Damien Hirst, an assemblagist, painter, and conceptual artist whose deliberately provocative art addresses vanitas and beauty, death and rebirth, and medicine, technology, and mortality. Considered an enfant terrible of the 1990s art world, Hirst presented dead animals in formaldehyde as art. He employed ready-made objects to shocking effect, and in the process he questioned the very nature of art.

ENVIRONMENTAL SCULPTURE

Environmental sculpture is intended to involve or encompass the spectators rather than merely to face them; the form developed as part of a larger artistic current that sought to break down the historical dichotomy between life and art. The environmental sculptor can utilize virtually any medium, from mud and stone to light and sound.

The works of American sculptor George Segal are among the best-known self-contained sculptural environments; his characteristic white plaster figures situated in mundane, authentically detailed settings evoke feelings of hermetic alienation and suspension in time. By contrast, the eerily realistic figures of American Duane Hanson, who was influenced by Segal, are usually displayed in such a way as to partake of, contribute to, and indeed often disturb the given exhibition environment. Other notable sculptors of indoor environmental works include the American artist Edward Kienholz, whose densely detailed, emotionally charged works often incorporate elements of the surreal, and Lucas Samaras and Robert Irwin, both of whom have employed transparent and reflective materials to create complex and challenging optical effects in gallery and museum spaces.

The larger context of the natural and urban outdoors has preoccupied another group of environmental artists. The controversial "earthworks" of Robert Smithson and others frequently have entailed large-scale alterations of the Earth's surface; in one notable example, Smithson used earth-moving equipment to extend a rock and dirt spiral, 1,500 feet (460 m) long, into Great Salt Lake in Utah (1970).

Artist couple Christo and Jeanne Claude have involved large numbers of people in the planning and construction of such mammoth alfresco art projects as *Valley Curtain* (1972). Their numerous "wrapped buildings" have been notable among urban environmental works of the past few decades. *The Gates, Central Park, New York City, 1979–2005* was unveiled in 2005. Stretching across 23 miles (37 km) of walkway in Central Park, the work featured 7,503 steel gates that were 16 feet (5 metres) high and decorated with saffron-coloured cloth panels. *The Gates* was on display for 16 days and attracted more than four million visitors.

American architect and sculptor Maya Lin is best known for her design of the Vietnam Veterans Memorial in Washington, D.C. Lin is also concerned with environmental themes. Her large environmental installations take their inspiration from the natural features and landscape of the Earth. In a series of "wave fields" (*The Wave Field* [1995] in Ann Arbor, Michigan; *Flutter* [2005] in Miami; and *Storm King Wavefield* [2009] in Mountainville, New York), for instance, she reshaped grass-covered terrain to resemble undulating ocean waves.

PUBLIC SCULPTURE AND PUBLIC SPACE

Starting in the mid-20th century, a shift occurred in public sculpture away from monumental works commemorating civic leaders or achievements to works that sought to interact with their urban settings and the people who dwelt in those settings. Examples include the massive Picasso statue installed in downtown Chicago in 1967, Calder's *La Grande Vitesse* (1969, Grand Rapids) and *Flamingo* (1974, Chicago), and Nevelson's *Sky Gate—New York* (1978). While some of this art was permanently installed, other works were temporary installations. For example, a 1967 exhibition of Tony Smith's sculptures at New York City's Bryant Park became the first of many art exhibitions in the city's public parks. Smith's often monumental sculptures, which he called "presences," are based on geometric principles and simplicity of form, fundamental characteristics of Minimalist art.

Public sculpture can take many forms. The work of Swedish-born American Pop-art artist Claes Oldenburg demonstrates several of these. In 1962 Oldenburg began creating a series of happenings, i.e., experimental presentations involving sound, movement, objects, and people. For some of his happenings Oldenburg created giant objects made of cloth stuffed with paper or rags. These interests led to the work for which Oldenburg is best known: soft sculptures. Like other artists of the Pop-art movement, he chose as his subjects the banal products of consumer life. An exhibition of Oldenburg's work in 1966 in New York City included, in addition to his soft sculptures, a series of drawings and watercolours that he called *Colossal Monuments*. While his early monumental proposals remained unbuilt, his *Lipstick (Ascending) on Caterpillar Tracks* was placed surreptitiously on the Yale University campus in 1969. This began a series of successes, such as *Clothespin* (1976) in Philadelphia, *Colossal Ashtray with Fagends* at Pompidou Centre in Paris, and *Batcolumn* (1977), provided by the art-in-architecture program of the federal government for its Social Security Administration office building in Chicago.

The public reception to public sculpture has not always been positive. American sculptor Richard Serra is best known for his large-scale abstract steel sculptures, whose substantial presence forces viewers to engage with the physical qualities of the works and their particular sites. One of Serra's key artworks, *Tilted Arc*, commissioned in 1981 by the U.S. government for Federal Plaza in New York City, brought heated discussions about its artistic purpose and its effect on the public space. The piece, which measured 120 feet (36 metres) long and 12 feet (almost 4 metres) high, was positioned in such a manner that movement through the plaza was impeded, thus forcing people to engage with the sculpture by walking around it to cross the plaza. After a public hearing in 1985 concerning myriad complaints about the piece and a subsequent challenge by Serra, the piece was destroyed in 1989.

Public sculpture continues to inspire discussion into the 21st century. The response to the Indian-born British sculptor Anish Kapoor's *Cloud Gate*—a 110-ton elliptical archway of highly polished stainless steel that was unveiled in Chicago's Millennium Park in 2004—has been overwhelmingly positive. On the other hand, his *ArcelorMittal Orbit* received more mixed views from the public. While some loved the 377-foot (115-metre) tower surrounded by a looping lattice of red tubular steel that was commissioned by the city of London for the 2012 Olympic Games, others considered it an eyesore.

CONCLUSION

Over time, Western sculpture has changed in many ways and can be classified as belonging to myriad movements and periods. As varied as these have been, each is an expansion of or reaction to the sculpture of earlier periods.

The aesthetic raw material of sculpture is, so to speak, the whole realm of expressive three-dimensional form. Sculpture may draw upon what already exists in the endless variety of natural and man-made form, or it may be an art of pure invention. It has been used to express a vast range of human emotions and feelings from the most tender and delicate to the most violent and ecstatic.

All human beings, intimately involved from birth with the world of three-dimensional form, learn something of its structural and expressive properties and develop emotional responses to them. This combination of understanding and sensitive response, often called a sense of form, can be cultivated and refined. It is to this sense of form that the art of sculpture primarily appeals.

GLOSSARY

alloy A substance composed of two or more metals or of a metal and a nonmetal intimately united usually by being fused together and dissolving in each other when molten.

arcadian Idyllically pastoral, especially idyllically innocent, simple, or untroubled.

capital The uppermost part of a column or pilaster, crowning the shaft and taking the weight of the entablature.

cire-perdue A process used in metal casting that consists of making a wax model (as of a statuette), coating it with a refractory (as clay) to form a mold, heating until the wax melts and runs out of small holes left in the mold, and then pouring metal into the space left vacant.

coiffure A style or manner of arranging hair.

colonnette A small column especially in a group in a parapet, balustrade, or clustered column.

commission To ask or hire someone to make a work of art.

cruciform Having the shape of a cross.

faience Earthenware decorated with opaque colored glazes.

frieze A sculptured or richly ornamented band; especially one forming the part of an entablature between the architrave and the cornice.

glyptic arts The making of carvings or engravings, particularly on precious or semiprecious stones.

kinetic sculpture Sculpture in which movement, whether by a motor or by natural forces such as the wind, is a basic element.

metope The space between two triglyphs of a Doric frieze often adorned with carved work.

modelling The shaping of a pliable material, such as clay or wax.

niche A recess in a wall, made especially for a statue.

nonrepresentational Representing or intended to represent no natural or actual object, figure, or scene.

personification The practice of representing a thing or idea as a person in art, literature, or so forth.

provenance The history of ownership of a valued object or work of art or literature.

relief A mode of sculpture in which forms and figures are distinguished from a surrounding plane surface.

rhetoric Language that is intended to influence people and that may not be honest or reasonable.

sarcophagus A stone coffin, particularly one from ancient times.

stucco A type of plaster used for decoration or to cover the outside walls of houses.

translucent Not completely clear or transparent but clear enough to allow light to pass through.

triglyph A slightly projecting rectangular tablet in a Doric frieze with two vertical channels of V section and two corresponding chamfers or half channels on the vertical sides.

BIBLIOGRAPHY

GENERAL

An excellent general history of world art is Hugh Honour and John Fleming, *A World History of Art* (1982; U.S. title, *The Visual Arts: A History*), which examines sculpture in relation to the other arts. H.W. Janson, *History of Art* (1962; 2nd ed., 1977), is also recommended. Among books that discuss sculpture of many periods, Ruth Butler, *Western Sculpture: Definitions of Man* (1975), is unusually valuable. So, too, is F. David Martin, *Sculpture and Enlivened Space* (1981). For the techniques of sculpture see W. Verhelst, *Sculpture: Tools, Materials, and Techniques* (1973); and Rudolf Wittkower, *Sculpture* (1977). The making of bronze sculptures, omitted from the latter, is brilliantly elucidated by Jennifer Montagu, *Bronzes* (1963, reissued 1972). Erwin Panofsky, *Tomb Sculpture* (1964), traces from ancient Egypt to about 1800 some of the major themes of one very important class of Western sculpture.

ANCIENT MEDITERRANEAN

Sculpture in the early civilizations of southern Europe is seldom studied separately, but it is featured in the following general works: John

Boardman, *Pre-Classical* (1967, reissued 1979); R.W. Hutchinson, *Prehistoric Crete* (1962); A. Arribas, *The Iberians* (1964); N.K. Sandars, *Prehistoric Art in Europe* (1968); and Spyridon Marinatos, *Crete and Mycenae* (1960).

GREEK, HELLENISTIC, ETRUSCAN, AND ROMAN ART

An authoritative and comprehensive account of ancient Greek art (which, for the most part, means Greek sculpture) is Martin Robertson, *A History of Greek Art* (1975). For a succinct introduction to sculpture only, see John Barron, *Introduction to Greek Sculpture* (1981, reissued 1984). For the Archaic period, G.M.A. Richter, *Archaic Greek Art Against Its Historical Background* (1949), is still valuable; a later volume, now standard, is John Boardman, *Greek Sculpture: The Archaic Period: A Handbook* (1978; corrected ed. 1991, reprinted 2007). For the so-called Classical period, Brunilde S. Ridgway, *Fifth Century Styles in Greek Sculpture* (1981); and John Boardman, *Greek Sculpture: The Classical Period: A Handbook* (1985; corrected ed. 1991, reprinted 1995) are good detailed guides. For the later periods, Margarete Bieber, *The Sculpture of* the Hellenistic Age, 2nd rev. ed. (1981) is highly useful. For the ancient literature on art, see J.J. Pollitt, *The Art of Greece 1400–31 B.C.: Sources and Documents* (1965). Etruscan sculpture is best discussed in Otto J. Brendel, *Etruscan Art* (1978). Sculpture features prominently in the most lively general books on Roman art: R. Bianchi Bandinelli, *Rome: The Centre of Power* (1970; originally published in Italian, 1969), and *Rome: The Late Empire* (1971); and Richard Brilliant, *Roman Art* (1974). Of more limited scope but great interest is Jocelyn M.C. Toynbee, *Art in Roman Britain* (1962). See also J.J. Pollitt, *The Art of Rome c. 753 BC–AD 337: Sources and Documents* (1966, reissued 1983).

EARLY CHRISTIAN AND EARLY MEDIEVAL

Good general surveys of the early Christian period that include some discussion of sculpture are Ernst Kitzinger, *Byzantine Art in the Making* (1977); John Beckwith, *The Art of Constantinople*, 2nd ed. (1968); André Grabar, *The Beginnings of Christian Art: 200–395* (1967, originally published in French, 1966); Steven Runciman, *Byzantine Style and Civilization* (1975); and Cyril A. Mango, *The Art of the Byzantine Empire 312–1453:*

Sources and Documents (1972). This last volume, together with Ernst Kitzinger, *Early Medieval Art* (1940; rev. ed., 1983), concerns also the early medieval period. Among more specialized studies of sculpture in the early Christian period, John Beckwith, *Coptic Sculpture* (1963); and Joseph Natanson, *Early Christian Ivories* (1953), should be mentioned. For general information on the early medieval period, see Peter Lasko, *Ars Sacra 800–1200* (1972); George Henderson, *Early Medieval* (1972); and George Zarnecki, *Art of the Medieval World* (1975). Valuable studies specifically on sculpture include George H. Crichton, *Romanesque Sculpture in Italy* (1954); Hermann Leisinger, Romanesque Bronzes (1956); Fritz Saxl, *English Sculptures of the Twelfth Century* (1954); and M.F. Hearn, *Romanesque Sculpture: The Revival of Monumental Stone Sculpture in the Eleventh and Twelfth Centuries* (1981).

GOTHIC

Many of the ideas expressed in this section of the book are treated at greater length in Andrew Martindale, *Gothic Art* (1967). General studies of Gothic art include George Henderson, *Gothic* (1967); Joan Evans (ed.),

The Flowering of the Middle Ages (1966, reissued 1984); and Johan Huizinga, *The Waning of the Middle Ages* (1924, reissued 1976; 12th Dutch ed., 1973). For the imagery of the period, the reader is referred to Émile Mâle, *The Gothic Image: Religious Art in France of the Thirteenth Century* (1958, reissued 1972; trans. of 3rd French ed., 1910), and *Religious Art from the Twelfth to the Eighteenth Century* (1949, reissued 1970; originally published in French, 1945). A useful anthology of the literary sources of the period is Teresa G. Frisch, *Gothic Art 1140–1450* (1971). For a general treatment of English Gothic sculpture, see Lawrence Stone, *Sculpture in Britain: The Middle Ages*, 2nd ed. (1972); for France, Marcel Aubert, *La Sculpture française au moyen âge* (1947); and for Italy, John Pope-Hennessy, *Italian Gothic Sculpture*, 2nd ed. (1972).

RENAISSANCE

There are numerous general books on Renaissance art, especially on Renaissance art in Italy, but sculpture is seldom adequately discussed in them. The best introduction to the sculpture is John Pope-Hennessy, *Italian Renaissance Sculptures*, 2nd ed. (1971). As a succinct guide to the sculpture in

Florence, the most consistently important centre in Europe at this time, Charles Avery, *Florentine Renaissance Sculpture* (1970), is recommended. Renaissance sculpture in northern Europe is discussed in Anthony Blunt, *Art and Architecture in France: 1500–1700* (1953); Wolfgang Stechow, *Northern Renaissance Art: 1400–1600* (1966); Gert von der Osten and Horst Vey, *Painting and Sculpture in Germany and the Netherlands: 1500–1600* (1969); and Michael Baxandall, *The Limewood Sculptors of Renaissance Germany* (1980). For Spain and Portugal, see George Kubler and Martin S. Soria, *Art and Architecture in Spain and Portugal and Their American Dominions: 1500–1800* (1959).

BAROQUE AND ROCOCO

The best brief general discussion of Western art of this period is Michael Kitson, *The Age of Baroque* (1966, reissued 1976), which includes some consideration of sculpture. For Italian Baroque sculpture, a better guide than Pope-Hennessy (above) is provided by the sections on sculpture in Rudolf Wittkower, *Art and Architecture in Italy: 1600–1750*, 3rd rev. ed. (1973, reissued 1982). Robert Enggass, *Early Eighteenth-Century Sculpture in Rome*, 2 vol.

(1976); and the first two volumes (1977 and 1981) of François Souchal, *French Sculptors of the 17th and 18th Centuries*, must also be mentioned. For 18th-century France, the sections by Michael Levey on sculpture in Michael Levey and Wend Graf Kalnein, *Art and Architecture of the Eighteenth Century in France* (1972), are excellent. For English sculpture, see the admirable account in Margaret Whinney, *Sculpture in Britain: 1530–1830* (1964). For Spain, Portugal, and Latin America, see Kubler and Soria (above); Harold E. Wethey, *Colonial Architecture and Sculpture in Peru* (1949, reprinted 1971); and Pal Kelemen, *Baroque and Rococo in Latin America* (1951).

NEOCLASSICISM AND THE 19TH CENTURY

An excellent general account of Neoclassicism, which includes much of value on sculpture, is Hugh Honour, *Neoclassicism* (1977). For England, see David G. Irwin, *English Neoclassical Art* (1966); Benedict Read, *Victorian Sculpture* (1982); Susan Beattie, *The New Sculpture* (1983); and Whinney (above). For France and Italy, see Gerard Hubert, *La sculpture dans Italie napoléonienne*(1964); Jane Van Nimmen and Ruth Mirolli, *Nineteenth Century French Sculpture* (1971), an admirable introduction; and Peter Fusco and H.W. Janson (eds.), *The Romantics to Rodin* (1980), also a good introduction. A superb general introduction— perhaps the only truly comprehensive one— to Western sculpture of the 19th century is H.W. Janson's contribution to Robert Rosenblum and H.W. Janson, *Art of the Nineteenth Century* (1984; U.S. title, 19th Century Art).

MODERN

The best books devoted to modern sculpture are Albert E. Elsen, *Modern European Sculpture: 1918–1945* (1979); Herbert Read, *A Concise History of Modern Sculpture* (1964); and Fred Licht, *Sculpture: 19th and 20th Centuries* (1967); Allen Kaprow, *Assemblage: Environments and Happenings* (1966); and Udo Kultermann, *The New Sculpture* (1968; originally published in German, 1967).

INDEX